W9-CXJ-884

"Can you imagine what our wedding reception is going to be like this time?"

Teddy asked with a grin.

"Teddy..." Quinn tried to head him off.

"Maybe we should get two rooms. One for your family and friends, and one for mine. And, Quinn, I want to pay for the whole thing. I can swing it, even though it might not turn out quite as ritzy as something your father would put together."

"Teddy!" Quinn strove to get a word in edgewise. She had to stop him right now!

"Hear me out," he went on. "I'll try to keep things as sedate as I can, but I can tell you my family won't believe it's a real wedding if they don't get to dance the tarantella at least once. And let me warn you, we're going to have to allow my father to sing."

Quinn pushed back her chair and got to her feet. It seemed the only way to cut him off.

Startled, Teddy looked up at her.

"We're *not* getting married again, Teddy!"

Dear Reader,

June . . . a month of courtship and romance, white lace and wedding vows. And at Silhouette Romance we're celebrating those June brides and grooms with some very special tales of love and marriage. Best of all—YOU'RE INVITED!

As every bride knows, you can't march down the aisle without the essentials, starting with *Something Old*—a fun-filled look at love with an older man—from Toni Collins. Gabriella Thorne falls for her boss, Adrian Lacross—a handsome and oh-so-charming . . . vampire. Can the love of a good woman change Adrian's fly-by-night romantic ways?

Something New was in store for prim-and-proper Eve Winthrop the day the new high school principal came to town. Carla Cassidy brings us the *irresistible* Brice Maxwell, who shakes up a sleepy Oklahoma town and dares Eve to take a walk on the wild side.

Linda Varner brings us *Something Borrowed* from the magical land of Oz! A tornado whisked Brooke Brady into Patrick Sawyer's life. Is handsome Patrick really a heartless Tin Man—or Brooke's very own heart's desire?

Something Blue is an unexpected little package from the stork for newly divorced Teddy Falco and Quinn Barnett. Jayne Addison's heartwarming style lends special magic to this story of a couple reunited by the miracle of their new baby.

Elizabeth August gives the final touch to our wedding bouquet with *Lucky Penny*. Celina Warley and Reid Prescott weren't looking for a marriage with love, but with luck, would love find them?

Our FABULOUS FATHERS series continues with an unforgettable hero and dad—Judd Tanner, in *One Man's Vow* by Diana Whitney. Judd is a devoted father who will go the limit to protect his four children—even if it means missing out on the love of one very special woman.

In the months to come look for books by more of your favorite authors—Annette Broadrick, Diana Palmer, Lucy Gordon, Suzanne Carey and many more.

Until then, happy reading!

Anne Canadeo
Senior Editor

SOMETHING BLUE
Jayne Addison

Silhouette
ROMANCE™
Published by Silhouette Books New York
America's Publisher of Contemporary Romance

If you purchased this book without a cover you should be aware
that this book is stolen property. It was reported as "unsold and
destroyed" to the publisher, and neither the author nor the
publisher has received any payment for this "stripped book."

For my husband—
Yes, I can still say I'm crazy in love....

SILHOUETTE BOOKS
300 East 42nd St., New York, N.Y. 10017

SOMETHING BLUE

Copyright © 1993 by Jane Atkin

All rights reserved. Except for use in any review, the reproduction
or utilization of this work in whole or in part in any form by any
electronic, mechanical or other means, now known or hereafter
invented, including xerography, photocopying and recording, or in
any information storage or retrieval system, is forbidden without
the permission of the publisher, Silhouette Books, 300 E. 42nd St.,
New York, N.Y. 10017

ISBN: 0-373-08944-9

First Silhouette Books printing June 1993

All the characters in this book have no existence outside the
imagination of the author and have no relation whatsoever to
anyone bearing the same name or names. They are not even
distantly inspired by any individual known or unknown to the
author, and all incidents are pure invention.

®: Trademark used under license and registered in the United States
Patent and Trademark Office and in other countries.

Printed in the U.S.A.

JAYNE ADDISON

was nineteen years old when she married, and her husband, Jerry, was twenty-six. They had an outdoor ceremony at Tappan Hill in Tarrytown, New York, featuring a breathtaking view of the Hudson River below. The August weather was spectacular, foiling the forecasters, who had all predicted rain. Standing beneath the trellis of roses, neither Jerry nor Jayne thought into the future as they lived the perfection of the moment.

That was many years ago. Now, they have a son entering a master's degree program, another starting law school and a nineteen-year-old daughter who is in college. Recently, Jayne's daughter told her she must have been crazy to have married at nineteen. "I was crazy," Jayne replied. "Crazy in love!"

Quinn Barnett on marriage:

I still think about marriage. Actually, I think about
it often. I see myself with a husband very much like
my father—naturally, younger and with more hair.
Teddy is the *antithesis* of my father. Teddy is impulsive,
spontaneous and glib. He wouldn't know a serious
thought if it ran him over. I know why I married
him. He absolutely bowled me over. I also know why
we couldn't make a go of it for more than a few
months. We just don't have anything in common.
We drove each other nuts.... What do I have to do
to stop being so unbelievably attracted to him?

Teddy Falco on marriage:

What can I say? I'm a fly-by-the-seat-of-my-pants
kind of guy. I never gave marriage much thought.
Then I saw her.... I knew, in that instant, that I was
going to make Quinn Barnett my wife. Maybe I
should have spent time courting her, instead of
sweeping her off her feet. I had her saying "I do,"
before she had the chance to draw a second breath.
We lasted a few months before her logical, inhibited
mind clicked in, and then we got divorced. Now
she's having my baby, making plans for us to
equally, but separately, parent our child. I've got my
own idea on that score. We belong together. All we
have to do is figure out how to get along. If I have to
turn myself inside out, I'll do it. I'm going to do
whatever it takes to get her back on cloud nine with
my wedding band on her finger.

Chapter One

"Miss Barnett," Carol, Dr. Wextler's receptionist, called out as Quinn got ready to put her coat on.

A very disoriented Quinn turned slowly at the sound of her name.

Carol, with her young and perky brunette appeal, smiled. "The doctor is going to want to see you again in four weeks. I suggest we set your appointment up now."

Quinn walked toward the front desk, carrying her beige-on-brown herringbone tweed coat. She nearly tripped on the Gucci wool scarf that she'd folded midway in the pocket of the Chanel coat when she'd hung it up.

Carol was flipping pages of a large white appointment book. "What day of the week is good for you?"

"Well...um," Quinn was having trouble thinking straight. "I'm pretty busy during the week. I teach."

Carol raised her eyes. "What do you teach?"

What did she teach? Quinn nervously flicked her blunt-cut ginger-blond hair back with her fingers. *You know what you teach....* "Music appreciation. I'm a professor at NYU."

"You're kidding! You don't look like a professor."

"Well, you see, I'm a cellist," Quinn said, as if that explained something.

"This is really a coincidence." Carol's cheeks dimpled. "My boyfriend is going to NYU. I think he's taking a course in music appreciation."

Quinn crossed her fingers under the fold of her coat. *Please don't mention his name and ask if I know him. I'm having a problem remembering my own name at the moment.*

Carol found the correct appointment page. "Saturdays are okay, right? Today is Saturday, and you don't teach on Saturdays, do you?"

"Yes, Saturdays... I mean, no, Saturdays... Saturdays are fine." Quinn stuck one hand in the pocket of her expertly tailored chocolate-colored wool slacks. Though she was making an effort, Quinn couldn't find the poise that ordinarily came unconsciously to her.

Carol had her pencil poised while her eyes scanned a calendar-lined page. "How is February nineteenth? We have openings at eleven, two and four."

"Eleven," Quinn replied. "Or two. No, I'll take the eleven."

"Okay, we'll see you then." Carol wrote Quinn's name in the eleven-o'clock slot and handed her an appointment card with the date and time. "Do you have your prescription and instruction sheet?"

"Yes." Quinn fumbled with her leather purse as she placed the card in one of the compartments. She put her coat on and swung the printed wool scarf around her neck, ready to brave the cold of January in New York.

The few people hurrying along Fifty-first Street and Park Avenue were huddled deep within their heavy outerwear. It took only a second for Quinn's face to start smarting from the wind chill. But Quinn wasn't feeling the discomfort. She stood still in astonishment as Dr. Wextler's announcement fully sank in. Never in her life had something this wildly unexpected happened to her.

The wind blew her straight hair into her face, and she put a hand up to keep it from her eyes. That action got her going. She walked to the curb, circumventing a block of grimy ice. The snow had been heavy so far this year.

She saw an unoccupied cab and stepped into the edge of traffic to hail it down. Missing it, she got splashed with cold, muddy water as a passenger car passed by.

It took Quinn ten minutes to get a cab. Twenty minutes later she was in her one-bedroom condo apartment in Gramercy Park.

She took off her scarf and, without the usual care that she gave her things, just let it drop on the narrow fruitwood table in the entry hall. She slipped out of her coat and deposited it right on top of her scarf. Pulling her white silk shirt free from the waist of her slacks, Quinn began unbuttoning as she walked across the gleaming parquet floor and the imported Swedish rug that was a swirl of chartreuse, yellow and white, past potted palms and philodendrons and airy rattan and wicker furniture with plump yellow-and-lime cushions. Her clothing fell to the floor in an hodge-podge behind her steps. She didn't even glance at the cello set before the only hard-backed chair in the room. Music wasn't going to soothe her rattled nerves. What she needed was a long soak in her tub. She needed to think.

Quinn's soft skin was pruned by the time she got out of the tub. She'd put herself through a long bout of unnecessary considering and reconsidering to arrive at what she'd decided right at the beginning was morally correct. But Quinn wouldn't have been Quinn if she hadn't thought it through over and over again.

Bundled in an oversized white chenille robe, Quinn sat down at the side of her bed and picked up her phone. Her nerves were still flying in a hundred and one different directions.

Teddy was expecting a call and he answered just after the first ring. He was sitting at the desk in his Soho loft, making arrangements for his newest protégés—a hip-hop trio—to do a summer tour of the East Coast.

"Yes," he said briskly, cradling the receiver between his right shoulder and ear while he continued to eye a column of numbers he was working on.

"Hi, Teddy. It's Quinn."

"Quinn?" He almost lost the receiver, and had to use his hand to kept it from falling.

Standing now, Quinn paced as far as her phone cord would allow. It didn't take much more than the sound of his voice to get her quivering, and since he couldn't see her, she let herself quiver without restraint.

"There's something that I need to talk to you about. Could we...ah...meet? Say tomorrow or maybe the next day? Or next week?"

No, answered his better judgment. He'd said to himself only this morning, as he had every morning since their divorce, that if he never saw Quinn Barnett again it would be too soon.

"What about now? I can pick you up in an hour. We can go for dinner." Grass didn't grow under his feet once he'd kicked his better judgment into the dirt.

Quinn hadn't considered that as a possibility. Her heart nearly stopped, then beat faster. Still, it did make sense to get this done quickly now that she had come to a decision.

"All right. In an hour." She willed her shivers to stop, and her mind to be sensible. She used to act like an adult, but that was before he'd burst into her life.

Teddy was prompt, though he could have used more time than the past hour to figure out if he didn't need his head examined....

Quinn put a hand to her racing heart, then took a deep breath before she opened the door to his knock. "Hi," she said, with her pulse beating all over the place.

He looked exactly the way she'd memorized him, standing before her exuding charisma, with his once-broken nose, his brown bedroom eyes, his dark, wavy hair. He practically defined sexuality in the almost cowboy boots and knocked-about brown leather jacket that served as his casual attire, and sometimes his dressy and business attire, too.

She'd suggested once that he buy a topcoat like the one her father wore. The suggestion hadn't gone over big.

"Hi," Teddy volleyed back after a long pause during which he tried to suppress torture number 3,000,089 before it came full-on.

"Well..." Quinn said. Her mind was mushy, but she did manage to reexamine a recent thought. Dr. Wextler's announcement wasn't the wildest thing that had ever happened to her. Teddy Falco was the wildest thing that had happened to her.

"Yeah..." Teddy hiked the collar of his jacket up higher. "Ready to go?"

Quinn turned back into her apartment to get a jacket from her hall closet.

Teddy walked in and took it from her as soon as she'd pulled one from a hanger.

"Allow me," he said, holding it open for her while he glanced around. Of all the issues between them, this condo of hers topped the list.

Quinn pivoted her back to him. His modulated courtesy had her bristling. She'd had enough experience with him to know that this was one of the ways he behaved when he was angry. Well, she had as much to be angry about as he did. He'd thrashed her as good as she'd thrashed him in the explosion that had ended their ridiculous marriage.

"Thank you," Quinn said, after buttoning the front.

Teddy gave a half-salute in recognition of one of her goddess looks, and walked back out to the hallway.

Not rising to his gesture, Quinn locked her front door with her key. She set exceptionally high standards of behavior for herself.

"How've you been?" he asked in the elevator.

"Fine..." With what was left of her resources, Quinn just about managed to ape his unflappable cool. "You?"

"Fine." He lied like a trouper.

Quinn trembled when he brushed her side as they came out to the street. She hoped he'd interpret her shivers as a response to the chill in the air.

"Cold?" he asked. He remembered how she was when she was warmed up. No one could say Teddy Falco wasn't a glutton for punishment.

"A little." Quinn tipped her chin and worked on governing the magnitude of sensations he created in her.

She searched diligently for more small talk as he led her a block away, to his leased Corvette convertible, with its now-closed roof. She couldn't come up with anything inconsequential.

He was rankled by her lack of reaction at seeing him. He didn't want to believe that she didn't feel any of the responses he was feeling. But then, that was another one of their problems. It was his personality to fling himself into his emotions. She needed to think and think some more before she allowed herself to decide how she felt—and even then she wasn't always certain.

Teddy broke the silence as soon as they were both seated in his car. "I thought we'd go to that Chinese restaurant you used to like on Pell Street. Unless you'd rather something else?" She was equally partial to Le

Cirque, but he couldn't have gotten a table there without booking weeks in advance—unless he used her last name. And that went against his grain.

Quinn nodded graciously. "That's fine."

Teddy stole a glance at her as he drove. There was something different about her, but it wasn't anything he could put his finger on. She looked as classy and cultured as usual. Her hair was sleek and shiny, her makeup was soft and understated, her clothes were impeccably structured to fit her slim shape. She had on black wool slacks and a heavy black wool blazer-styled jacket. He was thinking more about the pink cashmere sweater she had on underneath, with the turtleneck at the throat. She'd been wearing a barely-there pink dress the very first time he'd laid his eyes on her. Had it only been four months and three weeks since St. Thomas? It seemed to him that he'd known her the entire twenty-nine years of his life. Not that knowing her had anything to do with understanding her.

"What did you want to speak to me about?" He shot for the target. The wait was killing him.

Quinn kept her eyes trained straight ahead, but she was aware he'd turned his head her way. "I'd rather talk at the restaurant." She needed a little more time to work herself up to this. She was holding herself tight, wondering how he was going to take her news. She hadn't decided what kind of response she wanted from him.

"All right." Since he didn't have any other options, Teddy cooled his jets with overstrained patience.

Quinn snuck a glance at his profile, venturing a brief study of a sideburn, an ear, the thick dark hair that fell negligently on his brow. His head started to slant in her direction, but she quickly pulled her eyes away. Was what they had an attraction gone haywire? She'd been trying hard to diagnose it. It was something she'd failed to do at the beginning.

The tension between them was thick enough to be used as mortar to build a brick wall. "How's work?" he questioned, to fill the void.

"It's been a pretty easy semester so far." Her voice sounded squeaky to her ears.

"How's your Thursday-night practice going?"

She met with four other string musicians every Thursday night. She'd told him of her fantasy of playing professionally, and she'd told him of all her unsuccessful auditions. He had absolutely no feel for chamber music. She didn't have any feel for rock and roll, or rap, or that other music he liked. What did he call it? Hippity-hop?

"We've added another violinist to the group." She inserted that afterthought in an attempt to keep up her end of the conversation.

"Aha." He thought about her doing the limbo with him in St. Thomas. He could get her to be impertinent and sassy when he pushed hard enough.

They stopped for a red light. Teddy reached for a cassette he'd preselected and set it to play in his tape deck. He knew she could tolerate listening to jazz. His mind, however, stayed on the beat of the limbo, and the sway of her hips, and the way she'd laughed.

"Teddy, you're passing the garage," Quinn said, breaking into his reverie.

He had to circle the block to get back to the opening. He parked, and they walked in step to the restaurant, which was just down the street. It was early enough for them to get in and seated before the Saturday-night lineup formed.

"Where have the two of you been keeping yourselves?" Charlie Su asked, standing by their table, waiting to take their orders.

"We haven't been getting around much lately," Teddy responded for both of them. "Do you know what you want, Quinn?"

She wanted to fling herself in his arms, to forget that they just couldn't figure out how to get along with each other. "Hot and sour soup, and chow har kew."

Quinn opened her cloth napkin, rolled the silverware out and set the napkin on her lap. She performed without looking at him. Teddy worked his own napkin while his eyes measured her.

Quinn pulled in a gulp of air, fixed her hazel eyes upward and blurted, "I'm pregnant. I'm almost three months pregnant."

"What?" Teddy couldn't have been knocked more for a loop if the ceiling she was looking up at had just come down on his head. "What did you say?"

"I'm having our baby. I haven't finished thinking it through, but I do know that I am going to have the baby."

Teddy was thunderstruck, overwhelmed, elated. "A baby... Oh, Quinn..." The hard shell he'd been trying to build up as a defense against her cracked wide open, leaving him completely exposed.

She looked at him, tracking his joy, her heart in her throat. Maybe if they'd stayed in St. Thomas, become beach bums, and never returned to the real world...

His sexy brown eyes gleamed at her. "Have you told your parents yet?"

"Not yet." Quinn shook her head. "I thought you should be the first to know."

Teddy grinned. "I can just picture the expression on their faces when you tell them. They may be even more shocked than when you introduced me as your husband."

"It will be a close call." Quinn smiled back. She couldn't keep from responding to his grin.

Teddy groaned with amusement. "Boy, did they ever disapprove of me."

Quinn nodded. "You're forgetting that your family didn't like me any better." The disapproval of both their families had been one of many sore spots between them.

Teddy reached out for Quinn's hand, noticing only then that their soups were on the table. "Quinn, my family didn't dislike you. They just hoped that after a while you'd loosen up a bit. They didn't understand that you weren't used to a family that can fill a stadium on their own."

"They are bit much to an only child." And more demonstrative than she'd ever known people could be.

Teddy laughed softly. "Let's concede that it had to be difficult for both sides to deal with the fact that we got married after only knowing each other for two weeks."

Quinn smiled again, but her heart remained heavy. "I still haven't figured out how you swept me off my feet the way you did." Could there be any two people more incredibly wrong for each other?

He sent her an intimate message with his teasing eyes. "I told you about the Italian thunderbolt. When it strikes you don't stand a chance."

"Did that thunderbolt ever get you before?" Quinn asked, her voice subdued.

Teddy's eyes held a vulnerability that he didn't try to hide. "I've always fallen in *like* quite easily, but never in love... not the way it was with you. The minute I saw you, Quinn. I knew. Maybe not in my mind, but somewhere in my heart. Didn't you feel it the same way?"

"Yes," Quinn admitted openly, caught up with him.

A devilish grin lifted Teddy's mouth. "I loved that dress you were wearing. Did I ever tell you that?"

Quinn's smile became impudent as her mind drifted all the way back. "You told me that in the first minute we met, when you pulled up on your motorcycle and annoyingly interrupted me from picking out fruit at that open market."

He served her up a tantalizing wink. "I don't think you were that annoyed. You just thought I was handing you a practiced line of bull."

That was exactly what she'd thought. What in the world had he seen in her, anyway? She didn't see herself as more than ordinary-looking.

Teddy's gaze turned soft. "I'm still glad I didn't take no for an answer."

"Maybe we should have talked to each other more." Quinn sighed. "Get to know who we really were at the beginning."

"Talked?" Teddy kept his voice light. "I was having a hard enough time trying to keep us on top of the bike." His eyes became seductive. "I was a goner at the very first feel of you pressed against my back with your arms wrapped tight around my hips. I was whipping turns no sane man would make just to make you cling. Did you know that, Quinn?"

Her cheeks grew heated. "No." Quinn whispered her response.

Around them, chairs scraped, silverware clinked, and the aroma of ginger and garlic permeated the air. Charlie Su came up to their table and looked down at their untouched soups.

"Is there something wrong with the soup?"

"I'm going to be a father," Teddy said, smiling from ear to ear.

"Wow!" Charlie exclaimed. "Lots of luck to the two of you."

Quinn blushed again, but on the inside she still felt immeasurably sad. She needed to talk to Teddy about the future, not the past. That was the point of this meeting.

"I think the hot and sour soup might be a little too spicy for Quinn, anyway," Teddy told Charlie. "Just bring us our meals."

Charlie Su left with their soups before Quinn had the chance to object. The doctor hadn't cautioned her against spices. He'd only instructed that she take her vitamins and calcium pills, and watch that she didn't put on too much weight....

Quinn had a sudden, horrifying image of herself weighing two tons. Would Teddy still think she was attractive when she no longer had a figure?

"What were you thinking when you got on that motorcycle with me?" Teddy asked, wanting to keep her focused on St. Thomas.

Quinn looked away. "I don't think we should go over all that now."

Teddy's hand came out to gently touch her chin, turning her face back his way. "I don't want to give up St. Thomas, not one minute of it. Tell me what you were thinking that first day, Quinn. Please."

Against her common sense, knowing it was only going to make matters worse, Quinn capitulated to Teddy's devastating charm, and to the small ounce of spontaneity in her system that, until him, she hadn't known she even had.

For him, Quinn took a break from the argument going on in her head. "I had never allowed myself to be picked up before—and by a perfect stranger, no less. And I'd never been on a motorcycle. I was scared to death on both counts."

"Why did you let me pick you up?" Teddy asked, knowing the answer, as any lover would. It wasn't the words that were important to him. It was keeping that shine in her hazel eyes—drawing them back together, the way they'd once been.

She was being disarmed by his magnetism. "I wouldn't have if I'd given myself a chance to think," she answered honestly. "I guess it was being on vacation...thinking about turning thirty years old. It seemed the time to be unconventional. And it was daylight. And you said you'd stop following me around if I took one ride with you along the beach."

Teddy flashed his white teeth. "Quinn, you have three years to go before you turn thirty."

"*Just* three years," she said, a smile in her voice. "And I did need some excuse for myself."

Teddy lifted his water glass. "Here's to three years to being thirty, and you being unconventional." He took a swallow. "Why don't I get a bottle of wine? We can get some champagne later. Or shouldn't you drink?" His brow creased, and he thought about how much he had to learn.

"Drinking liquor is out," Quinn answered.

Teddy poured tea into each of their cups. He raised his. "Here's to the beach in St. Thomas. I kept my word. It was just one ride."

Her eyes clung to his. She couldn't help herself. Lifting her tea, she toasted him back. "It was a very long ride. All day and all night. I never watched the sun rise before. It was breathtaking."

Quietly Quinn evaluated the pattern of life.... If she'd kept to her plan to tour the museums of Europe with friends, as she did ever summer, she wouldn't be sitting here now. If Teddy hadn't decided that St. Thomas was a perfect place to try out a rapper client of his, their paths might never have crossed. Fate was quite unpredictable....

Teddy watched Quinn, intimate thoughts having a field day in his head. She still took his breath away.

Charlie Su set their dinners down on the table.

"Eat," Teddy ordered gently as Charlie Su walked off. "Keep in mind, you're eating for two."

Smiling the candid smile he adored, Quinn lifted her chopsticks. "Eating for two is a cliché. I'm not supposed to gain more than eighteen pounds."

Teddy's brown eyes made a tour of all he could see of her across the table. His appreciative notice stayed a little long on the delicate swell of her small breasts. He didn't have any objection at all to the way she fit against his palms. "You could use a little fattening up. If my mother had her way, she'd see to it that you put some meat on your bones."

Quinn secured a coated shrimp and sent Teddy a playful glance. "I thought you liked my shape." She was naturally slim.

"I do." His tone was tender.

For several seconds, Quinn let Teddy see the depth of feeling she had for him in her gaze without allowing any of the complications and reservations get in her way. Then, struggling, she pulled herself past the moment. She squared her shoulders, but her face still had a look of utter susceptibility. She should have spoken to him on the phone. She shouldn't be with him now. He was so hard to resist.

He read her reaction. Sometimes he could read her so well. Other times he couldn't read her at all. "You have seen a doctor, right?" He brought them back to the present giving her a breather from the past.

"Today."

"Did he give you a due date?" Teddy picked up his chopsticks and started to eat.

"July twentieth, give or take a few days either way." She was going to be a mother sometime in July.... It was unbelievable!

A father! Teddy thought about it. He was going to be a father!

"Can you imagine what our wedding reception is going to be like this time?" he asked with a grin.

Quinn tried to head him off. "Teddy..."

"Maybe we should get two rooms. One for your family and friends, and one for mine. And, Quinn, I want to pay for the whole thing. I can swing it, though it might not turn out quite as ritzy as something your father would put together."

"Teddy..." Quinn strove to get a word in edgewise. She had to stop him.... She had to stop him right now!

"Hear me out," he said, not giving her an opportunity to speak. "I will try to keep things as sedate as I can, but I can tell you my family won't believe it's a real wedding if they don't get to dance the tarantella at least once. And let me warn you, we're going to have to allow my father to sing."

Quinn pushed back her chair and got to her feet. It seemed the only way to cut him off.

Startled, Teddy looked up at her.

"We're not getting married, Teddy," Quinn said, and sat back down.

"We're not?" He studied her askance.

Quinn shook her head, her eyes watering. "We can't do to each other again what we've already done. We have nothing in common. We get on each other's nerves. I know we're drawn to each other, but it must be because of some kind of chemical mix-up. I know I can't explain it."

Teddy's frustration showed. "We're having a baby. I'd say that gives us something in common."

"We do have that," Quinn agreed, dashing errant tears from her eyes. "And we've had this really nice time this evening, sitting here and reminiscing. We do fine when it comes to our physical attraction to each other—"

Teddy jumped in. "We have more than a physical attraction."

"I don't want to fight with you, Teddy. I can't help it if I need to intellectualize my behavior. You're who you are. I'm who I am. Not that there's anything wrong with who you are. I admire who you are. I tried to become a little more devil-may-care for you, even if you didn't notice."

He could have said something glib to her at this point, but he held it in. Maybe she had tried and he hadn't noticed. But then, he hadn't done much trying to change himself. And here he was looking to run roughshod over her again, when he knew she needed to think things through more, even though with Quinn that could be ad infinitum. . . .

He took a few deep breaths. It tore him up watching her wipe away tears. "You know me—one stupid impulse after another. We'll take it day by day. We'll just enjoy knowing we're having a baby, and we'll see where it leads. Is that better?"

"Yes." Quinn breathed a sigh. It wasn't better, just the only way.

"Come on, eat your dinner. I want a fat, roly-poly kid." Please, Teddy prayed, let me find the way to get it right with her this time.

Chapter Two

Teddy reached out blindly to pick up the phone on his nightstand. He'd been sleeping.

"Hello." His voice was gruff.

"Did I wake you?" Quinn asked, reprimanding herself.

Teddy pulled the receiver closer to his ear and rubbed at his eyes with his free hand. "No. I'm up." He looked over at the clock on the nightstand. It was almost 8:00 a.m.

"Mmm..." said Quinn, knowing he was lying. "I've been thinking most of the night."

Teddy smiled. Was there a more compulsive thinker than Quinn? "I've been thinking myself. I've been thinking about you and thinking about becoming a father."

Restless, Quinn sipped from a glass of milk. "We did real nice together last night."

"I thought so myself." He kept an even tone, fighting himself to let her set the pace.

Quinn caught her breath. "Do you think we could get together again today and talk?" She wasn't throwing caution to the winds. She already knew there wasn't any Cinderella ending out there for them. But they did have issues to resolve.

Teddy bit down on his knuckles to keep the high sign he'd been about to verbalize from her ears. "Sure. How about I come over and take you for breakfast?"

"I'll come to you." She was already dressed in heavy jersey jogging pants and a sweatshirt. Her hair was held back from her face with a braided silk headband.

"Quinn, it would be easier for me to come to you. I have a car."

"I feel like getting out in the air, and I'm sure I won't have any trouble getting a cab. There are usually more than enough of them around on Sunday mornings."

"All right." The new Teddy Falco didn't persist though he felt she was being obstinate. The old one would have pushed until he had gotten his way.

"See you soon," Quinn said, and set her receiver back into its cradle.

Pulse racing, Teddy bounded from the bed and did forty push-ups on the floor in record time. Then he headed for a quick shower, smiling and puffing.

Quinn stamped snow from her boots on the mat outside the door to Teddy's loft while she waited for him to answer her knock. Her face was all rosy, her hair was full of static when she pushed back the hood of her down parka.

Teddy pulled open the door. "Hi," he said casually.

"Hi," Quinn returned with a trace of natural hauteur as she entered.

Teddy, ever the maverick, had considered greeting her bare-chested, with just his jeans on, hoping to ignite her physical attraction to him. He might have gotten away with it, saying he'd just come out of the shower. In the end, he'd reconsidered playing it down-and-dirty with her. Instead, he'd pulled on a loose-fitting oatmeal knit sweater with his jeans and boots. He wanted her to love him for himself... or at least the self that she wanted him to be. It was too bad, Teddy thought, that he didn't own a smoking jacket. He'd bet her father had a closet full of them, though he didn't smoke.

"Let me give you a hand with your boots," he said, after collecting her jacket and hanging it on the coatrack in the entry.

Not objecting, Quinn sat down on a dark green painted bench close by. Teddy bent down in front of her as she put her foot out. She looked down at his dark hair, still damp and glistening from his shower, and had to struggle to keep her hands in her lap. He smelled wonderfully of soap and spicy after-shave.

Her eyes roamed over his impressive shoulders and flexing muscles. He was the sexiest man alive, and her body chemicals were getting enticingly mixed up all over again.

He set her boots aside and watched her wiggle circulation back into her toes, which were covered with white athletic socks. He didn't think it showed, but just that innocent movement of hers had him in a sweat.

He raised his eyes when she stood. It didn't matter what she wore, she always looked like she'd just stepped out of a page in *Vogue*. "I have decaf dripping away. I'll make us some omelets," he said, drawing in a heavy fix of her perfume. She wore Obsession. It was apropos.

Quinn turned to pull a small spiral-bound notebook from the pocket of her parka. She had a definite reason for visiting him this morning. At least that was what she was telling herself.

Teddy sent a glance to her pad, but he said nothing as he led her through the large living room and into the kitchen. The scent of Obsession wafted his way. He tried to breathe shallowly.

Quinn walked over to the white counter that dominated the center of the room. It served as Teddy's kitchen table. She sat down on a black painted stool. The kitchen was designed all in black and white. He'd offered to let her redecorate. She most definitely would have if they'd lasted together more than three months.

Teddy went to work at the stove. Quinn remembered when she'd conceded—in the first week they'd lived here together—that he was the better cook. She hadn't learned much about cooking growing up.

Within minutes Teddy had served them both mushroom omelets and toast. Quinn poured them each coffee with a hand that wasn't quite steady. She was aware as she brought her cup to her lips that he was using the fresh-ground decaffeinated blend that she had introduced him to. It was a relief to her that he had continued to stay away from all the caffeine he used to drink.

They ate, relaxed, or at least appearing that way to each other. Quinn didn't open her spiral pad until after Teddy had placed their empty plates in the sink.

"What I did," Quinn began, "is jot down some thoughts on how I feel we should handle the situation."

"Are you talking about your pregnancy?" Teddy asked carefully, then took another sip from his second cup of coffee.

"Yes. I feel we should decide ahead of time how we are going to behave with each other. I didn't think we'd be seeing each other again after our divorce, but now that's all changed." Her hair, cut along the line of her jaw, fell like a curtain over her cheeks as she bent her head. Unconsciously she adjusted her headband, pulling her ginger hair tighter off her forehead.

Teddy struggled not to look amused. Leave it to Quinn to try and map this out. "Would you suggest I take notes?" he teased, keeping his face straight.

Quinn rolled her lips together, signaling that she was thinking his offer over. He found that particular habit of hers endearing. "That's a good idea," she answered, not discerning his amusement.

Teddy got up from the counter and found a piece of paper and a pen. With his back to her, he smiled the smile he'd been stifling, getting it out of his system. "Shoot," he said, sitting down again, ready to write.

"The first issue we should address is the attraction between us...." Quinn paused. Rolled her lips.

Teddy's grin came before he could stop himself as did the quip that followed. "I can't imagine anyone but you trying to analyze attraction."

Quinn drew herself up until her back was ramrod-straight. "I should have known that you wouldn't take any of this seriously."

Teddy quickly adjusted his expression. "I am taking this seriously. Start again. I'll behave. What about the attraction between us?"

Quinn scrutinized Teddy for a long, doubtful moment. "I see it as a problem," she said inadequately.

That, he thought, might just be the understatement of all time. "Do you have a solution?" If she did, he couldn't wait to hear what it was.

"I don't know if you'd call it a solution. It's more a suggestion."

"I'm listening." He held her gaze for a good second before hers skittered away.

"The best I could come up with is that we ignore it." Bracing herself, Quinn waited for him to say something flippant.

Teddy wrote on his piece of paper. Item 1... Attraction—Ignore it. He turned the paper around to face her.

Quinn glared at him in annoyance. "I thought after last evening that we'd be able to work this out. I should have known better."

"Give me another chance, Quinn." Teddy feigned a chastised demeanor, but there wasn't any sham in the way his heart ached. He had everything at stake here.

He'd do anything he had to do to work it out with her. "What's the next item?"

Scrupulously Quinn avoided his eyes. "We can't go on to the next item until we've discussed the first one."

"Fine. Let's discuss it. Do you want to go first?"

She didn't have the vaguest idea of what to say, let alone how to handle it. It hadn't seemed to require this kind of pinpoint examination when she'd written it down. It was something they both should just have understood.

Teddy turned his paper around again. "How about we leave this item to the end?" He wanted to keep the peace. "We'll come back and discuss it."

Quinn forged ahead, glad to be off the hook for the moment. "Item two has to do with telling your parents and my parents. And..." She hesitated again.

Teddy waited impatiently.

Quinn continued. "And it seems to me that it's important that both our families understand that you and I are going to be equally involved with parenting. You do want to be equally involved?"

Teddy squared off with his eyes. "You can take that for a fact."

Quinn took a fortifying breath. "As equal as possible, living apart...which brings me to my next item..."

Teddy interrupted. "Before you move ahead, I have a thought on item number two. I should go with you when you tell your parents. I want them to see right off that I'm going to be involved. And you should come with me when I tell my family."

Quinn rolled her lips. She didn't want to go with him when he told his family, but she did appreciate the idea of having him at her side for support when she dealt with hers. They were not going to be overjoyed. "All right," she agreed.

"When should we do it? And which family goes first?" He didn't like the second half of this item at all—the part about parenting separately.

"I think we should tell my parents first. After all, your parents are already grandparents."

"When did you want to tell them?"

Quinn rotated her lips.

He knew her well enough to know that she was planning to procrastinate. "Why don't you give them a call now and tell them we're coming over?" The way he saw it, she was only agitating herself additionally by putting it off.

"We have all day, Teddy. We can even do it this evening." She found it very annoying when he pushed.

"Not if we're going to get both families in. I think it's only fair that we tell them both on the same day."

"We can do them both today. We'll go see my parents in the afternoon and yours this evening. I really want to work out the rest of my list with you."

Teddy flashed her a grin. "Don't tell me that we have to decide now which college we're going to send him to."

Quinn couldn't stop her smile. "It could be a girl." The look she gave him was sassy.

Teddy raked a hand through his hair. A girl! Imagine that... "If it's a girl, we lock her in a closet as soon as she becomes a teen...maybe sooner, since she's going to have half my genes. And we keep her away from any guy that resembles me."

She gave him another of the smiles he'd earned. "Was your father stricter with your sisters than he was with you and your brother?" Teddy was one of five. She'd met them all.

"I'd say he was strict with each of us in different ways, but my sisters could always wrap him around their little fingers. He did torture the life out of every boy they ever brought home, and he worried a lot that Frankie and I were going to turn into punks."

Quinn became wistful, thinking about growing up an only child. It seemed quite probable that her child would grow up an only child, as well. "Have you started dating again?" Her inquiry followed the direction her thoughts had taken.

The question jarred Teddy. "No." He winced, then regarded her with a brooding expression. "Have you been dating?"

Quinn shook her head.

He'd never gotten as far as seeing her with someone else, not even in his worst moments. The potential of that happening struck him full-force. The smile he gave her this time was forced. "Let's drop the middle of your plan for a moment and get back to item number one."

"The attraction between us?" Quinn asked, surprised by the sudden change in his tone of voice.

"Yes, the attraction between us." He pinned her with his gaze.

She was all tense again. "I'm concerned that if we see each other on a regular basis one of us might get carried away."

"That's a possibility." He was vexed, but he was trying not to show it. "There's also the possibility that we might get carried away at the same time. A double whammy, so to speak.''

Quinn's chin came up. ''Don't think that I don't know you're being glib.''

''I'm not being glib. I'm just stating the possibilities.'' What did he have to do to make her understand that there was more than a physical attraction between them? They were soul mates, even if it was like pulling teeth to get her to figure that out.

''We could limit the amount of time we spend together,'' Quinn theorized obliquely. She didn't miss the irony behind her remark. She was the one who had initiated this second go-around. It was dumb of her not to have thought this all through a little longer.

Teddy got to his feet. He was too agitated to stay seated. He stood with his feet spread wide. ''Just so there's no misunderstanding, I want you to know that I intend to be as much a part of your pregnancy as I intend to be an equal parent to our child.''

Quinn's gaze veered from Teddy to the countertop. ''How do you suggest we handle it?''

He wanted to tell her that they should be having this conversation in bed, curled up together, and then start learning how to be with each other, one day at a time. Only that hadn't worked with her during their marriage.

''As you suggested before, we could ignore it,'' he volleyed back at her.

Quinn tried to think of a fast, pithy return to cover her own stupidity in making that remark earlier. But she couldn't come up with anything. ''Are you saying that it's that simple?''

"Considering the fact that you were the one who wanted the divorce, I wouldn't think it would be that hard for you."

Quinn grabbed the pen Teddy had left on the counter and scribbled hard on her notepaper.

Teddy came up behind her to see what she'd written. She'd jotted down *IGNORE IT* on the page in big block letters.

"I'd say this is a first," Teddy bantered tightly. "We've actually come to an agreement on something."

Defiantly Quinn nodded her head.

Teddy flattened the palms of his hands on the countertop and pitched his upper body toward her. "Let's get a little more specific. What exactly are we ignoring? Did you want to get into any particular behavior?"

Quinn was getting more than a little agitated. "I know you think you're irresistible, but..."

"You think so, too, or we wouldn't be having this conversation."

Quinn's eyes sparked. "Would you please stop crowding my space?" His nearness and this conversation elicited vibrations. She was having a hard time not squirming in her seat.

Teddy straightened and backed up a little. "You know what your problem is? You're repressed. I don't have a problem admitting that I find you irresistible."

"I am not repressed. I am trying to be adult. We should be mature enough at our ages to handle attraction."

"I can handle it as well as you can."

Quinn watched his mouth angle in a smile. She couldn't believe that he had the audacity to find this a laughing matter. "I doubt that." She forced herself to remain composed. If nothing else, lack of sleep had her at a big disadvantage.

Teddy played it out. "I'll tell you what... You show me your stuff and I'll show you mine. In case you want to jot that down, it comes under the heading of challenge number one. I have a feeling that I may come up with some more."

Quinn looked at him wearily. The give-and-take they were having had her plumb tuckered out.

Teddy stuck out his hand. "Deal?"

Quinn shook his hand and pulled free quickly. She got to her feet, ready to leave. "I'm going home."

"Oh, no. Not so fast. We just made a bargain. You're not going to be living up to your end if you dodge me every chance you can."

Quinn was steamed. "What are you suggesting? That I spend twenty-four hours a day with you?"

"No," Teddy responded, though he would have liked to put that kind of spin on it. "I'm saying that I'm not going to let you dash away every time I get too close to your sensibilities."

"Did I ever mention that I thought you were an egomaniac?"

"Among other things." He grinned.

The ringing of Teddy's telephone saved Quinn a comeback.

"Hold that thought," Teddy quipped, going over to pick up the extension on the wall.

"Hello," he answered.

"Teddy, it's Lisa."

Teddy mouthed over to Quinn, "It's my sister, Lisa." Then he got back to his call. "What's up, honey?"

Lisa sniffled. "Oh, Teddy... Johnny and I broke up.... Can I come over? I need some hugs...."

"I'll come by and get you. Are you home?"

"Yes, but don't come. If Mom and Daddy see you come and get me, they'll know something is up, and I don't want to talk to them yet."

"All right. You come right over. Take a cab. I'll pay for it when you get here."

"See you soon." Lisa sniffled again and hung up.

"Lisa and her boyfriend, Johnny, broke up," Teddy explained to Quinn after he got off the phone.

"She's coming over?"

"Yes. She needs some comforting." Teddy turned to the sink, rinsed their breakfast dishes and stacked his dishwasher.

Quinn started for the hallway to get her boots and coat.

Teddy reached Quinn at the kitchen door. "Don't go," he said.

"Lisa is coming to cry on your shoulder. She doesn't need me around."

"I don't want you to leave." He extended a peace-offering smile. "Please, Quinn."

Damn you, Teddy, Quinn said to herself, standing there melting at the way he said please.

"Tired?" he asked, looking her over.

"Yes." The reminder drew a yawn.

"Go lie down and take a nap."

Her eyes flew up at the suggestion of getting into his bed... putting her head on his pillow... smelling his

scent.... Just the thought, and her breathing became
rushed....

He knew she was thinking about his bed. "The bed
in the guest room is all made up," he said off-
handedly.

She was glad he hadn't deduced where her thoughts
had just gone. He would have said something provoc-
ative. "A nap does sound tempting."

"Would you like me to tell you a daytime-nighttime
story?" The gaze he gave her was quintessentially
male, and was intended to do a teasing job on her
senses.

"I don't think so." Quinn looked him smack in the
eye. "I'm much too vulnerable to you when I'm tired.
Put down on your paper to cut the charm when I'm
tired."

Teddy grinned. "Me, give up an advantage? No
way."

Quinn laughed. "Promise you won't let me sleep
too long."

"I promise," Teddy responded, promising more
with his heart as Quinn left the kitchen. Maybe he
wasn't making as much headway as he would have
liked, but he was moving forward.

Quinn slept less than an hour. She came out of the
guest room into the living room to find Teddy and Lisa
sitting together on Teddy's red sailcloth couch. Lisa,
who had the same warm brown eyes as her brother,
and the same dark hair—hers long and curled by a
perm—looked startled when Quinn stepped into the
room.

"Quinn..." Lisa looked from Quinn to Teddy. "I didn't know you were here. Did the two of you get back together?"

"No," Quinn answered. "We're not back together. Not that way."

Teddy's heart took a nosedive when he heard Quinn equivocate about their relationship. "We've just become friends," he said, looking at Quinn. That might have been part of their problem. They'd been lovers, but they'd never given themselves a chance to be friends. Not for the first time since Quinn had entered his life, Teddy denigrated himself for always being in a rush.

Lisa teared up. "I wish Johnny and I could be friends, but I don't think that's going to happen. Maybe the difference is that he's the one who broke it off." Lisa raised tragic eyes to Quinn's sympathetic gaze.

Teddy slung his arm around Lisa's shoulders again while motioning with his eyes for Quinn to sit down.

Quinn sat opposite Lisa and Teddy on a love seat that was covered in blue and white stripes.

"I have to admit that my pride is hurt, too," Lisa said.

"Had you been fighting?" Quinn asked.

"No." Lisa shook her head slowly and stuck out her left hand. "He gave me this bracelet for Christmas. It's beautiful, isn't it?"

"Yes." Quinn leaned forward to admire Lisa's gold bangle bracelet. Her eyes met Teddy's as she lifted her head. They hadn't had Christmas together. Her lawyers had walked their divorce papers through court, with her father pulling some strings, just a week before. She'd spent Christmas Eve at the Russian Tea Room with a small group of other socialites—their idea of a homey private dinner party. She'd tried to beg off, but her parents, who had also been invited, wouldn't hear of it. They'd meant well, thinking that being with friends would cheer her up. If anything, it had made her more melancholy. The entire holiday season had been one long melancholy blur.

Teddy looked away from Quinn. Christmas had been a disaster for him. He'd been with the family in Bensonhurst. It had been a double celebration this year, with his parents welcoming a new grandchild into the fold. The house had been wall-to-wall people, but he'd felt entirely alone. He shouldn't have been there, putting a damper on everyone's good time.

What if she was right? What if there were too many differences between them for them to bridge the gap?

Lisa gazed up at her older brother. "Thanks, Teddy, for not saying that I'm too young to know about love. That's something that Mommy and Daddy would say. I'm eighteen years old, but they still treat me like a baby."

Teddy smiled tenderly at Lisa. "You're always going to be the baby of the family, no matter how old you are. How about something to eat now? A cup of coffee?"

"I still don't want anything to eat. What I want is to get my mind off Johnny."

"How about going for a walk?" Quinn suggested. She'd walked miles herself in the throes of depression—not that it had helped. "Or we could go shopping." She'd also tried that exercise in futility.

"It's Sunday," Lisa said. "There's not much open." She wanted an activity—anything.

"There should be some stores open in the Village," Quinn said. The occasion had never arisen for her to spend any time with Teddy's siblings on a one-to-one basis. En masse, they were more than she could handle.

"Don't the two of you have other plans?" Lisa asked, glancing from Quinn to Teddy.

"We were just going to be lazy for now," Teddy answered. "I'll tell you what. I have some work I should get to. The two of you go, and when you've finished shopping, come back and I'll drive you both home." Teddy got to his feet to pull his wallet from the back pocket of his jeans. "It's on me, and I want the both of you coming back here with packages." He fished out his American Express card.

"That's not necessary," Quinn objected.

"Let me ease my guilty conscience." Teddy smiled. "I'd pay anything to get out of going shopping."

Lisa, with her first smile of the day, took Teddy's credit card. "I'm going to freshen up and then we'll go. Okay, Quinn?"

"Okay," Quinn answered, feeling a lot as she imagined an older sister would feel.

"Thanks," Teddy said after Lisa went to the bathroom.

"You don't have to thank me." Quinn's head was tipped back so that she could look up into Teddy's eyes.

"We're still on for later today, right?" he asked.

"Yes. My parents first, then yours."

"Will you tell Lisa that we're having a baby while you're out?"

"I don't know." She hadn't thought about it.

"It's all right with me if you want to."

"I'll see."

Teddy's grin came quick. "Quinn Barnett being spontaneous . . . Maybe I should come along. It's going to be hard for me to believe unless I see it with my own eyes."

"I can be spontaneous," Quinn rejoined. "Especially if I plan for it."

Chapter Three

Quinn's mother was startled to see Teddy walk in with Quinn, but the elegant mien with which she carried herself saw Edith Barnett through with just the barest stumble.

Quinn had called to say she was coming by, and she had mentioned that she was bringing a friend. Quinn bet her mother was wondering when she and Teddy had become friends.

Edith extended both her hands to Teddy after giving her daughter a delicate hug.

"It's so nice to see you, Teddy." Edith smiled tactfully, with only a slight blink of her gray eyes.

She was a dainty woman, not at all long-legged like her daughter. Her professionally colored ash-blond hair was brushed stylishly off her barely lined face. She might have passed for younger than her late fifties if she didn't dress in such matronly styles. Today she wore a dusty rose blouse, a straight but not shapely black tweed skirt, and plump-heeled black-and-white spectator pumps.

Teddy gave both of Edith Barnett's cool palms a slight squeeze. "It's nice to see you." He'd never quite figured the protocol when greeting either of Quinn's parents. Was he expected to bow or kiss a hand?

"Where's the senator?" Quinn asked, passing her coat to Phillip, the butler, who was standing by.

"Your father is on the phone in the study," Edith replied.

Teddy removed his leather jacket and gave it over to Phillip's care.

Phillip took off with both coats after exchanging a warm smile with Quinn.

Edith turned to her daughter. "Quinn, why don't you take Teddy into the library? I'll see if your father is finished with his call."

Teddy and Quinn watched Edith graciously exit the wide center hallway of the Sutton Place duplex apartment. Teddy was guessing that the senator was going to need some preparing for his daughter's guest.

"How are you doing?" Teddy questioned after following Quinn into the library.

She was a wreck. Her heart was clamoring. Her mouth was dry. But in her parents' home Quinn always adopted the modulated manner in which she'd been reared. She wouldn't have thought of behaving any other way.

"I'm fine," she responded, but made the mistake of looking directly into Teddy's concerned eyes. "They'll be shocked, but they will be okay with it," she added in advance support of her parents.

Teddy nodded laconically, biting back a comment.

Impulsively Quinn touched his forearm. "I know what you're thinking, and you might be right. But when you say something about my family, it makes me feel threatened and I get defensive. I really don't want to be defensive with you...."

Teddy's heart cracked against the wall of his chest. It was the first time she'd been this open with him. And it was a revealing experience for him to see deeper into her feelings. He thanked whatever presence of mind had kept him from tossing her some of his jive.

"Would you like something to drink?" Quinn stepped over to a marble-inlaid cart that displayed a large silver tray set with glasses, an ice bucket, a decanter of sherry, a decanter of Scotch and a decanter of rye.

"Nothing for me." Teddy sat down on a heavy brocade couch. He glanced at the fireplace, which was filled with burning logs.

"There's ginger ale or club soda." Quinn continued formally.

Teddy shook his head while his eyes took a new inventory of her. She'd changed from her jogging attire of the morning to a long avocado wool skirt, a simple sweater that matched, and flat-heeled black suede boots. It always seemed to him that she chose muted tones for herself when she knew she was going to be around her parents.

He'd made a few concessions, as well. He still wore boots, though ones that were less western in appearance, and he'd replaced his jeans with charcoal-gray slacks, his slouchy sweater with a sport shirt in a lighter shade of gray. He wondered if unconsciously he hadn't tried to imitate her.

Quinn poured herself half a glass of ginger ale, swallowed it in four sips and then sat down on the same sofa as Teddy. She put a wide berth between them.

Teddy gazed around. Books in shelves lined the room, which was large enough for the Yankees to play the Mets in. A gracefully curved staircase led to a second-floor balcony, where there was even more reading material.

Teddy turned his eyes back on Quinn. He tried to imagine her sitting in this room, curled up on a couch or in a chair, reading. What kind of stories did she like?

Growing increasingly aware of Teddy's close scrutiny, Quinn sought a diversion. She lifted a miniature statuette of an elephant up from the mahogany cocktail table before them. "My mother collects elephants," she said, toying with it nervously, tipping him off to her inner turmoil.

"That makes it easy to shop for a present," Teddy said wryly, thinking that if this were a contest a judge would be hard-pressed to pick out which one of them was more tense.

"My mother has hundreds of them, all with their trunks up. It's bad luck if their trunks are down." Quinn's valiant attempt at small talk ended on that note.

Teddy couldn't think of anything to say.

A long six minutes later, William and Edith Barnett entered the room.

Quinn and Teddy stood and came around from the cocktail table, keeping a discreet distance between them.

The former New York state senator greeted his ex-son-in-law with a handshake. "Good to see you."

"Good to see you, sir." Teddy exerted exactly the same amount of hand pressure he was receiving.

"Hi, Princess." William Barnett gave his daughter a loving buzz on her cheek.

"Senator." Quinn swapped nickname for nickname with affection.

"What are we all standing for?" the senator asked. "Edith, would you like a sherry? Quinn . . . ? Teddy, what would you like to drink?"

"Nothing for me, Daddy," Quinn answered.

"Me neither," Teddy returned, choosing *knee-ther* over *nye-ther,* wishing for an ice-cold beer—right from the bottle, of course.

"I'll have a sherry, dear," Edith replied, sitting down on a matching couch opposite the one Quinn and Teddy had staked out. Quinn and Teddy took their seats again.

The senator strode over to the bar cart in his wing-tipped shoes, with their mirror shine. His navy suit was all sharp creases. His white shirt perfectly starched. His dark blue tie hardly a contrast, though if one looked closely there was a pattern worked in with maroon threads.

He fixed a sherry for his wife, and a neat Scotch for himself and came over to join the group.

Phillip entered with a tray of hors d'oeuvres and set it down on the cocktail table.

"I wish the two of you would stay for dinner," the senator said as Phillip walked out.

"We can't this evening," Quinn answered, sorry that she'd let Teddy talk her into dealing with both their families in one day. Hers was enough. . . .

Edith studied the amber liquid in her small crystal goblet between sips. The senator polished off his single-malt Scotch, put his glass down and, as was his habit, smoothed the sides of his silver-gray hair. He was predisposed not to disturb the strands on top, which were combed with precise intent to cover a patchwork of balding.

"Mom, Dad . . ." Quinn began, and then had to pause to clear the fog in her throat. "I'm pregnant."

Edith's eyes blinked twice in rapid succession when Quinn dropped her bombshell. A look of shock whipped across the senator's face.

"You're having a baby," Edith repeated, her eyelids keeping pace with her voice, which had turned staccato.

"Yes." Quinn nodded.

The senator, drawing himself up in his seat, took over. "I suppose the two of you are planning to remarry?"

Quinn met her father's eyes squarely. "No."

Teddy thought he heard a collective sigh of relief from the elder Barnetts. "But I do intend to be an equal parent to our child," Teddy said, laying his cards out on the table.

The senator cut the deck. "Exactly how is that going to work?"

"That's for Quinn and me to decide," Teddy answered tightly.

"I am not looking to usurp your role." The senator was just as controlled. "Our child is having a child, and we have a right to be concerned."

"Why don't you move back home, Quinn?" Edith suggested brightly, hoping to cool the male tempers in the room.

Quinn pressed her hands, palm over palm, on her lap. "Mom, I know that you and Daddy mean well, but it was hard enough for me to become even a little independent. I'm still working on it, and I won't give that up."

Teddy looked at Quinn. He'd never thought of her having to fight to be independent. Perhaps it wasn't that easy being born with a platinum spoon in one's mouth, having the pleasures in life handed over on a gilt platter.

The senator studied his daughter. "Princess, we just want you to know that we're here for you in any way that you need us."

Quinn sighed. "I know that, Daddy. I'd really like you both to be happy that you're going to be grandparents."

"We are happy," Edith rushed to assure her daughter. "Aren't we, dear?" She turned her head to her husband.

William Barnett's focus was on Quinn. "I'd be happier if I knew how you are planning to manage."

Quinn sat fixedly on the edge of the couch. "I'm going to manage the same way other single women manage with a child."

The senator went over to the cart for another Scotch. He spoke to Quinn over his shoulder. "The last thing your mother and I want is to make you upset. We just want you to understand the practicalities involved in rearing a child."

Teddy was close to losing it. "Sir, I hope you're not suggesting that Quinn abort our child."

The senator looked horrified, as did his wife. "We are certainly not suggesting that." The senator came back to his seat with his drink.

Edith tried to mediate again. "We only want to understand your plans. I'm having trouble understanding how you both intend to parent our grandchild. Are you thinking of shifting the baby between the two of you on a daily basis?"

Teddy pushed his way in. "That is something Quinn and I will discuss between ourselves."

The senator shot Teddy a fighting man's look. "I know that you think that Mrs. Barnett and I don't like you, but that is not the case."

You could have fooled me, Teddy said to himself.

The senator zeroed in on his daughter again. "You don't have to worry about financial support. I suggest we sell the Gramercy Park condo that your grandmother left you and get you something larger. Did you want to continue to work for a while?"

Teddy fumed. "Any financial support that Quinn needs will come from me."

Quinn reacted heatedly. "My apartment is large enough for me and the baby, and I intend to work. The two of you can stop trying to take over."

The senator glared at Teddy, blaming him for Quinn's upset. Teddy glared right back, redirecting the blame.

Again Edith made an attempt to defuse the scene. "When are you due, dear?"

Quinn took a long breath. "Mid-July. I've been to see Dr. Wextler."

"I'm so glad you're using Dr. Wextler." Edith saw the Park Avenue doctor for her own gynecological exams. "I'm terrible at counting. How far along are you?"

"Three months," Quinn answered.

Edith smiled. "I didn't start showing with you until well into my sixth month. I have a feeling you'll stay small, too."

Teddy and the senator gave up their staring contest to look over at Quinn.

Quinn blushed. "I think I show just a little bit already. I'm not sure I'm going to like being fat."

Teddy felt a lump growing in his throat. He hadn't thought of the changes going on inside her body until now, or the way they might affect her.

Stretching across the couch, Teddy took Quinn's hand. "You're always going to be beautiful, Quinn. Always." He didn't care what her parents thought of their relationship. Hell, he and Quinn couldn't figure it out themselves.

Quinn's cheeks turned scarlet again. "Thank you, Teddy," she said self-consciously, taking her hand from his. She appreciated his effort to make her feel special, but this wasn't the time or the place to be giving her a compliment. She was embarrassed in front of her parents.

Teddy bared a wrist to check his watch. "We should be going." He wanted to get her out of here before the pragmatic-minded senator struck again.

Quinn swallowed hard at Teddy's suggestion that they be unpardonably rude. They couldn't possibly cut their visit this short.

"Well, if you have some place you have to be." The senator got to his feet, looking relieved to dismiss them.

"Teddy and I agreed to tell his family about the baby the same day we told you. That's why we have to go," Quinn said, rushing to explain.

"That's only fair, dear." Following her husband's lead, Edith gave her daughter a leave-taking hug without much of a clasp.

The senator walked from the room to summon Phillip to get their coats.

In no time at all, Quinn and Teddy found themselves out the door. Quinn didn't catch her breath until they were stepping out of the elevator down in the lobby.

"They're not ogres," Quinn said, using her Sutton Place voice, as they walked by the doorman.

Teddy looked straight ahead. "I'm not passing judgment."

Quinn knew that wasn't the truth. "Yes, you are."

"I'll take you home" was Teddy's response.

Quinn clutched her coat underneath her chin, raised her face to Teddy and drew in cold air. "I agreed that we'd do both our families in the same day."

"Don't be stubborn. I'm letting you off the hook." He ran his arm around her waist as they headed for his car.

Quinn removed Teddy's hand from her person. "I wish that you wouldn't treat me like I'm a porcelain doll. Really... There are times when you and my father are quite alike.''

Teddy wanted to balk at Quinn's attack. Instead, he offered up a borderline laugh. "I don't think your father would approve of your even linking our names together in the same breath.''

Quinn's back was up. "You told your parents we were coming for dinner and that we had something to tell them. That's what we are going to do.''

"Whatever you say," Teddy retorted as they reached his car. He opened the passenger door and saw her in.

They traveled the east side of the city, through the skyline of lower Manhattan, over the Brooklyn Bridge and into Bensonhurst without any further discussion. Quinn knew Teddy was more than a little vexed. She hadn't meant to take out her agitation on him. Why did they have so much trouble reacting sensitively to each other?

Teddy parked on the street in front of his parent's two-story, semi-detached brick home. His brother, Frankie, had his car on the driveway.

"Do you think Lisa is home?" Quinn asked as Teddy opened her door. She was looking for an ally. They'd struck a chord together that morning.

"Probably," Teddy grunted shortly as they walked the slate path to the front steps.

"I hope she won't feel slighted that I didn't tell her we're having a baby when we were shopping.''

"The Falcos don't slight easy." He was letting her know that she had found the right button to push on him.

"Teddy..." Quinn stopped in her tracks. "I'm sorry."

Teddy contemplated the sorrowful look in Quinn's eyes. "You're forgiven," he said, amazed at how easily she could thaw him. "I can still get you out of here without a commotion."

"I want to tell them." Quinn tried her best to smile. "I'm okay with it...sort of."

Teddy grinned, the encounter with her parents somehow almost forgotten. He pressed a hand to Quinn's neck behind her upturned collar. It felt very good to Quinn to have the pressure of Teddy's vigorously masculine touch back.

"I'll take the lead this time," Teddy said before he gave the front door a one-two knock. He opened it and ushered Quinn in.

Teddy's oldest sister Nancy's two youngsters were the first to spot Teddy and Quinn.

"Uncle Teddy!" the fraternal twin girls squealed in unison.

Teddy bent low and opened his arms to catch the adorable chestnut-haired six-year-olds as they ran up to him. "I didn't see your father's car outside," Teddy said, almost smothered by their hugs.

"Mommy and Daddy dropped us off. They went out. Nana and Poppy are watching us," blue-eyed Stephie explained.

Dark-eyed Kim added, "Poppy is going to play cards with us later. Do you want to play?"

"Not with you two cardsharks," Teddy laughed, straightening up. "You girls remember Quinn."

The two nodded.

"Should we still call you Aunt Quinn?" Stephie, the more outspoken of the two, asked innocently.

Immediately feeling beleaguered, Quinn darted a glance to Teddy. She hadn't thought about the kids in the family being told about their divorce.

Teddy wanted to finesse the situation. "Well . . . ah . . ."

Quinn decided to answer for herself. "I like being called Aunt Quinn."

Teddy smiled at Quinn's response, though he cautioned himself not to make too much of it. "Where's Uncle Frankie and Aunt Lisa?" He unzipped his leather jacket while Quinn unbuttoned her coat.

Stephie made a face. "Aunt Lisa is in her room being a pill. She said she doesn't want to talk to anybody. Uncle Frankie is getting dressed for a date."

"Nana and Poppy are in the kitchen," Kim put in. "Nana made sauce with meatballs, and sausage and spareribs. Poppy wants to taste, but Nana won't let him. Do you want to watch TV with us till dinner is ready?"

"Aunt Quinn and I are going to go visit with Nana and Poppy." Teddy hung up his jacket and Quinn's coat in the hall closet. "Ready?" he whispered to Quinn.

Quinn nodded, concerned that her voice might sound shaky. She was worried about the reception she was going to receive from her former in-laws.

As it turned out, Quinn needn't have been concerned. Connie and Anthony Falco greeted her effusively and as if she were still a member of the family.

"You look so nice," Connie said a second time, wiping her hands on the front of the terry apron she had tied over a cotton housedress. She was a short, full-figured woman with an olive complexion. Her hair was a cap of wavy pepper and salt, cut short to be easy to care for.

"Come sit down. We made the meatballs you said you liked." Beckoning to Quinn, Anthony Falco held out a chair at the kitchen table.

"What we?" Connie turned indignant brown eyes on her tall, thin husband. "*I* made the meatballs she likes! *You* watched!"

Anthony defended himself, sitting down next to Quinn. "Who ran to the store because you were out of oregano?"

Teddy grinned and then affected an injured expression. "Remember me? I'm one of your sons. Don't I rank a fuss?"

Connie looked her oldest son over, beaming at him as only a mother could beam. "Why did you give Lisa your credit card?" she chided, but there wasn't any real recrimination in her voice. "That girl doesn't have any space left in her closet."

Connie turned to Quinn. "Lisa couldn't understand how you could resist buying something."

"I guess I didn't see anything I needed," responded Quinn.

Teddy shot a look at Quinn. He'd blundered in the morning, offering her his credit card, but he hadn't understood then how she felt about being independent. Had she thought he was acting sexist? Was he sexist?

Connie stirred the meat in the thick red spaghetti sauce. "I think Lisa is late for school every morning because she has too many outfits to try on. She can't decide what to wear."

Teddy put a lid on the frustration he'd been designing for himself. He wouldn't ever tell Quinn to go shopping on his credit card again. "Did Lisa speak to you about her problem?"

"She spoke to us." Connie Falco sighed theatrically.

Anthony Falco made an expressive gesture with both his hands. "I made a mistake saying she was too young to know about love. She didn't want to hear that."

Frankie whipped into the kitchen, dressed snappily in a light blue turtleneck, dark front-pleated slacks and tassled loafers. His cologne nearly drowned the pungent aroma of tomatoes, garlic and herbs. "Hi, Quinn. Hi, Teddy."

"Hi, Frankie." Quinn smiled at the shorter, quirkier version of Teddy.

"Hey, Slick," Teddy bantered. "How's things going? You start at the car dealership yet?"

"I started last Monday, and it's going pretty good. This could be a career."

"My offer is always open," Teddy said. "You can come in with me anytime you want."

"I want to find my own angle," Frankie told him with a smile.

Anthony Falco kneaded the back of his neck. "Not that I'm counting, but this must be the tenth angle you've tried. How many angles do you think there are out there?"

"Anthony!" Connie sent her husband a look. "Leave him be—"

Frankie picked up a spoon from the counter and tasted his mother's sauce.

"Get out of there." Connie Falco took the spoon from his hand. "Sit down. I'll make you a plate."

"I don't have time."

"What time are you coming home tonight?" Anthony Falco was still sizing up his twenty-seven-year-old son.

Frankie smiled. "Not late."

"Tomorrow is a working day," Anthony Falco reminded him.

Frankie grinned. "I knew I shouldn't have moved back home."

"Sit down. You have time for one meatball," Connie insisted.

"I've got a date for dinner."

"You'd better air yourself out first," Teddy teased. "The girl you're taking out might keel over."

Frankie countered, "You get married and you forget that's the whole point." As soon as the rejoinder was out, Frankie realized his mistake.

Self-conscious, Quinn reddened.

Teddy groaned.

Anthony Falco shooed Frankie away. "Go, before you put your foot in your mouth some more."

"Sorry," Frankie mumbled, and took off.

The awkwardness and embarrassment Quinn had been fearing suffused the kitchen.

Connie and Anthony Falco's response was to bustle around. Anthony stuck his head in the oven to check the baked ziti. "Do you think you put on enough mozzarella?"

Connie bent down next to her husband. "It's perfect. Since when don't I put on enough mozzarella?"

At a loss, Teddy scanned Quinn, feeling protective but utterly useless. It was all his fault for riding her into this predicament. He should have told his family alone.

Quinn cast her eyes aside, blaming herself for everyone's discomfort. If she hadn't wanted Teddy with her when she'd told her parents, she wouldn't be here making everyone tense.

There was a ring from the front doorbell.

"That must be Fran and Sonny," Connie said.

Glad for an excuse, Anthony hurried out of the kitchen to let his brother-in-law and sister-in-law in.

Connie called after her husband, "Tell the girls that dinner is ready, and see if Lisa is going to make an appearance."

"I wish you had mentioned that Aunt Fran and Uncle Sonny were coming for dinner." Teddy exhaled a taxed breath. He loved Aunt Fran and Uncle Sonny, but Quinn hardly needed more company.

"It's Sunday. They always come for dinner on Sunday."

"Can I help with something?" Quinn asked, more uncomfortable just sitting. She'd met Teddy's Aunt Fran and Uncle Sonny once, at a party Teddy's parents had thrown to announce their marriage. There were scads of Falco relatives. Quinn couldn't tell one face from another, but some of the names had stuck in her head.

"You can get the antipasto from the refrigerator, and there's two bottles of soda and a bottle of Chianti. Teddy, take the baked ziti out of the oven while I get the sauce in a bowl.''

Quinn stepped to the refrigerator, with its side-door freezer, as if she were walking on eggshells across the shiny brick-patterned vinyl floor. Teddy tried to catch Quinn's eyes to telegraph a sign of apology, but she was too uptight to allow herself to look his way.

Within minutes the kitchen was filled with people. Even Lisa decided not to miss dinner, broken heart and all.

Aunt Fran gave Quinn a lively embrace, recognizing her. Quinn was daunted by the exuberance, though she ventured to return most of the hug. She was anxious not to look like a stick or come off as standoffish.

Behind Quinn and Teddy's back, Connie gave Fran a don't-ask-me shrug, raising upward palms in answer to her sister-in-law's unspoken question.

"How's the music business?" Uncle Sonny asked after giving Teddy a punch to his shoulder.

"Good, Uncle Sonny," Teddy smiled.

Aunt Fran stood by, a head taller than her husband, ruffling Teddy's hair. "Are you still traveling so much?" she questioned.

Before Teddy had the chance to reply, Anthony Falco broke in. "When isn't he running? I don't know what he's doing, but he's running."

"Dad, traveling is part of the business," Teddy smiled. "I'm going to be flying to Japan tomorrow. I have a group starting in concert there."

Quinn's eyes flew to Teddy.

Teddy answered the question in Quinn's upset gaze. "I'll be gone for a month." If there was a way he could have gotten out of it, he would have. But there wasn't.

"Are we going to eat?" Anthony Falco prodded. His mouth had been watering all afternoon for his wife's special sauce.

There was a shuffling of bodies and chairs. Teddy made certain that Quinn sat next to him. Lisa took the chair at her brother's other side. Aunt Fran, sweaters swaddling her almost emaciated frame, sat between the twins. Connie and Anthony took their places at either head of the table. Uncle Sonny folded the substantial corporation that bulged above his belt into a chair opposite Quinn.

Rapid table chatter progressed along with the meal. It was all a blur around Quinn. She picked at her helping of antipasto but forced a smattering of ziti and three meatballs down her throat until she couldn't eat a drop more. Just before the table was cleared to make ready for dessert, Teddy got to his feet. "Quinn and I have an announcement to make." Everyone except Quinn lifted their eyes. "Quinn and I are having a baby.... Before anyone asks, we haven't decided to get married again."

Connie Falco hit herself on the top of her head. "She's having your child and you're not going to marry her? What have I done wrong? Anthony, do something with him!"

Anthony banged a fist on the marbled Formica table. "Your mother is right!"

Aunt Fran piped in. "It's a different generation. Who understands them?"

Teddy reissued his statement. "I said we—*we* haven't decided to remarry."

Uncle Sonny tossed his input into the melee. "A man is a man. A man knows his responsibility."

"Excuse me..." Quinn said, trying to straighten things out.

Lisa began to cry. "All men stink...."

"Not now, Lisa." Anthony Falco flourished his hands.

Lisa looked at her father. "I don't mean you, Daddy. Or you, Uncle Sonny."

"What? I stink?" Teddy asked.

"Not as a brother," Lisa replied sheepishly from the hot seat she'd created for herself.

"Are you going to have a boy or a girl?" little Stephie asked Quinn.

"I don't know," Quinn answered. She was getting a headache.

Kim screwed up her cute face. "I don't want to have boy babies."

Teddy took the floor again. "I'd like you all to listen carefully. I am not shirking my responsibility. I am going to be a parent to my child."

Temple throbbing, Quinn vigorously nodded her head. "We talked it over and we decided that we shouldn't get remarried just because we're having a baby."

Taking turns, Connie and Fran pumped Quinn for information. Quinn answered questions about her doctor, her due date and whether or not she'd experienced morning sickness, which she hadn't.

Teddy reached for the bottle of Chianti and filled his glass for the third time.

"In my day—" Connie Falco raised an expressive hand "—you stayed in the hospital almost a week after giving birth. Now they send you home in two days, maybe three." Connie went on to detail each of her pregnancies, upstaging Aunt Fran, who had only two children.

In growing stupefaction, Teddy absorbed every new piece of information. Muscle cramps? What kind of muscle cramps? Was Quinn supposed to jog?

The table got cleared. Cheesecake and coffee were served. Lisa took her slice of cake to her room. Stephie found the deck of cards that Nana kept in one of the kitchen drawers. Each of the adults took a turn at playing go fish with the twins.

An hour later, Quinn had her coat on and Teddy was holding open the front door. Quinn felt her elbow firmly clasped as Teddy steered her toward his car. Quinn allowed herself to lean unguardedly into his strong side.

It seemed to take forever for the heater to warm the car. A light snow began to fall, and then it turned to sleet as they drove into the night with the headlights throwing oblique stretches of luster ahead of them.

Quinn sat shivering, admitting to herself what had been just a threatening eye-opener to her the entire past month. She couldn't live with him, but she didn't know how she could get along without him. And he was going to be leaving tomorrow for Japan.

Teddy found a parking space just up the block from Quinn's condo. She waited for him to come around and open her door. He helped her out and used his arm to tuck her close as they walked gingerly on the treacherous concrete. The snow was freezing as it touched the ground.

They rode the elevator up to Quinn's apartment on the third floor of the five-story building. Neither could find words for the other, even in the privacy of the lift.

Quinn unlocked her door with shaky fingers. Pushing the door just partially open, she turned and looked into Teddy's face. "Do you think I could borrow your shoulder for a second?" She was all too aware of how much she wanted and needed his nearness.

Teddy tapped his left shoulder, just over his heart. "This one's available to you for the next forty or fifty years. I need the other one to hold up a phone."

Quinn pressed her warm forehead to cold leather, drawing in Teddy's wonderfully unique male scent. "This doesn't mean anything, of course." She didn't want to confuse their relationship any more than it was already confused.

Teddy dropped his hands back to his sides, because they'd been about to pull her body closer to his.

Quinn took a step back and looked up at him again. "Japan, huh?"

"Yeah." His eyes locked on her. The hell with her restrictions, he decided. He was damned if he did and damned if he didn't, anyway.

In one swift motion, Teddy put his mouth over Quinn's and took control.

Quinn's mouth opened in surprise, and she reeled against him. Teddy fell back against the wall, taking her with him. Quinn put one hand to Teddy's chest, intending to push herself away. Her mind scrambled to remind her that this wasn't going to do either one of them any good. Teddy gripped her hand, captured the other, and brought them both up around his neck.

His tongue sought and hers greeted, and he moved her against him in sexual rhythm. A soft moan of abandon rose from Quinn's throat. She couldn't fight him.... She didn't really want to....

Teddy didn't know where he got the willpower to end it, but he did know as he released her that he was checking himself in the nick of time.

Quinn nearly toppled without Teddy holding her. She gripped the knob on the door to steady herself. Breathless, she could do no more than stare up at him.

"That didn't mean anything, either," he said, matching her stubbornness.

Sad and yearning, Quinn watched him walk briskly away.

Chapter Four

Teddy placed his suitcase and garment bag in the trunk and closed the lid. He kept the gift-wrapped box with him as he got into his car. He set it down on the passenger seat and inserted the key in the ignition, praying under his breath that the motor would kick over. The car had sat unused in frigid temperatures for three and a half weeks. He put his foot to the gas. The Corvette instantly jumped to life.

A layer of ice glazed the windows, freezing out visibility. Leaving the car idling, Teddy got out and scraped the windshield and the back window. The air was crisp and blowy and carried the odor of refined fuel. Overhead, jets circled in holding patterns, impatient to land, while others taxied in revved anticipation of soaring the sky. Five p.m., Teddy estimated, had to be the busiest hour at Kennedy Airport.

Back behind the wheel, Teddy blew into his hands. He ran his palms briskly over his thighs, drawing friction from the light flannel of his navy-blue slacks. He'd forgotten to leave his gloves unpacked.

He pictured Quinn. He knew he should call her first, not just drive over. Only he hadn't liked the way their phone calls had gone all the time he'd been away. Sure, she'd asked him all the right questions and answered his. Quinn wouldn't be Quinn without her sterling good manners. She just hadn't been anything more than succinct.

With a grimace of annoyance with himself, Teddy shifted into Drive. She'd given him no more than he'd deserved. He'd acted like such an idiot with her right before he'd left—not that there was anything particularly novel about that.

"Who's there?" Quinn asked, startled, when her doorbell rang. She wasn't expecting anyone.

"Teddy." He had the gift he'd bought her under his arm.

Quinn's pulse took a giant leap. Feeling awkward, her heart doing zigzags, Quinn fumbled as she worked three locks to open the door for him.

They stood absorbing each other with their eyes, not moving.

"Hi," Teddy finally said when he thought he could breathe again.

"Ah...hi..." Quinn was defenseless. She'd had no opportunity to build up the resistance she might have worked up against him if he'd given her notice.

His gaze left her face, and he glanced down her figure, seeking visual evidence of the tie that bound them. But he couldn't detect any sign of her pregnancy within the large white cashmere sweater she wore over a long, wavy plaid skirt.

Quinn's eyes stayed on Teddy's face, looking at the collar of his leather jacket, turned up at his neck, at the dark black hair that needed a trim. He looked wonderful to her.

"You said you wouldn't be back until the end of next week." She had one hand on the door, the other on the jamb, unintentionally blocking the entry to her apartment.

Teddy smiled easily, reacting to the warm expression on her face. They were doing much better in person than they had over the phone lines.

"Does that mean that you aren't going to let me in now?" he kidded.

"Oh..." Quinn blushed, stepping back so that he could enter.

Teddy pressed the door closed behind him. Again they stood looking at each other. His insides were trembling as badly as hers.

"Is it okay if I say that I missed you?" he asked, propped against the foyer wall, feet spread.

Quinn leaned against the opposite wall. "I missed you, too," she answered with her heart, not thinking past the here and now. It was the same way for her in this moment as it had been in St. Thomas, when she hadn't been able to think of any reason at all not to marry him. Love was all that counted. Except that was back then....

Teddy fought like hell not to take her in his arms as they stood disarmingly close in the narrow hallway, her scent filling his nostrils.

They spoke at the same time.

He remembered the gift he was holding. "This is for you."

"I was just on my way—"

"What?" Teddy straightened up to his full height.

Quinn took a side step. "I was just getting ready to go out."

"Where are you going?" He still had the gift under his arm.

"I'm meeting friends for dinner and a concert." Her hands fluttered. "I wish I could get out of it, but they're probably on their way by now." She really did wish she could get out of it.

Teddy nodded. "This is for you." This time he handed her the box.

"You didn't have to." All butterfingers, Quinn nearly dropped the package.

"Do you have time to open it?" He was doing his best not to let his disappointment show.

"Yes." She walked into the living room and sat down on a plump-cushioned wicker chair. Her legs were all shaky.

He followed her, but didn't sit.

Quinn tipped her face up toward him. She had a stranglehold on the box on her lap. "Would you like to go with me tonight? I happen to have an extra ticket. My friend Caitlin was supposed to go, but she called me today. She's got a bad cold."

"Who else is going?" He wanted her alone, not in a crowd.

"You know them. They're part of my chamber music group. Allison Richards, Travis Crane and Mitchell Logan."

He'd never made her friends his friends.

"A concert, huh?" He thought about it for a second.

"Beethoven . . . his complete works for cello and piano." Quinn felt it was only fair that she let Teddy know what he was letting himself in for.

"I'd like to go." He was willing to put up with Beethoven, and any of his cronies, if it scored him some points.

Flabbergasted by his agreement, Quinn ripped into the wrapping paper and opened the box. One at a time, she pulled out three kimonos, one pink, one blue, and a white one embroidered in silver.

Quinn smiled with delight. "Teddy, they're beautiful. Thank you." She stood and held the pink one in front of her, interpreting his message. "Pink for a girl. Blue for a boy. And white?"

"Just to knock around in." The shopkeeper had called it a wedding kimono, but he wasn't going to spring that on her yet.

"Oh..." She wanted badly to give him a thank-you hug, but was afraid to give herself permission. "I'll just hang them up, and then we really should get going. We won't get seated in the East Room for dinner past six-thirty. Travis will be impossibly petulant if we have to deviate from our plans."

Teddy grinned. "I wouldn't want to get Travis petulant."

"Are you sure you want to go?" she asked, still boggled.

"I'm sure," Teddy answered winsomely, enjoying her skepticism. This was a brand-new ball game. The old rules didn't count.

Quinn gave Teddy one more beguiling glance and
then took the kimonos to her bedroom. Teddy
watched the swagger of her skirt as it swayed just
above the ankles of her brown suede boots. His mind
traveled a deviating path to her plan for the evening,
and he groaned inwardly before setting himself back
on course. Beethoven, he admonished himself, think
Beethoven....

They met with the other members of Quinn's mu-
sical group in the lobby of Carnegie Hall. Like Quinn,
the harmonious three had been born into old money.
Mitchell Logan came from a long line of politicians.
Travis Crane's family was into Manhattan real estate,
as was Travis. Allison's father was the third in a di-
rect line of Richards men to own and occupy a seat on
the New York Stock Exchange.

Allison was the first to outwardly react to Teddy's
unexpected appearance. "It's great seeing you," she
said sincerely. She was the same age as Quinn, trim
and attractive, with a soft-featured face that was un-
defended by makeup.

"It's good to see you," Teddy responded, and
placed a light kiss on her cheek. She was a poetess.
He'd read some of her poetry while he'd been married to Quinn. He hadn't been able to catch Allison's
drift, but he figured she was good at her craft. She'd
had two volumes of her poems published.

Allison took the opportunity to murmur, "Congratulations" into Teddy's ear.

Teddy smiled. He was pleased, and not at all surprised, that Quinn had told her their news. She was
Quinn's closest friend and confidante. By the same

token, Teddy gathered from the way that Allison had whispered that neither Mitchell or Travis had been made aware. That part bothered him. He wanted Quinn to shout it from the rooftops. It didn't settle him any knowing that she wasn't going to be able to keep it a secret for too long.

Mitchell Logan, Esq., switched the gray topcoat he was holding to his left arm. He stuck his right hand out to Teddy.

"Mitchell," Teddy acknowledged, exchanging a handshake while he checked out Mitchell's brass-buttoned navy-blue blazer, gray slacks, white shirt and striped tie.

Grudgingly Teddy conceded that women would find Mitchell Logan, attorney at law, a terrific catch if they were lured by muscular definition, thick sandy hair, blue eyes, power, prestige, and classiness beyond classiness. Mitchell Logan was exactly the kind of man that Quinn's parents would have welcomed as a son-in-law. Of that, Teddy was sure!

Travis Crane, who would have been handsome if not for his thick bifocals and thin lips, shook hands with Teddy in turn. Then he made a peevish remark about not getting to the East Room in time.

Allison checked her watch and assured Travis that they were going to make it.

"Quinn, you do have the tickets, right?" Travis checked.

Quinn smiled. "Yes, Travis."

"Dinner is going to be Dutch treat," Quinn insisted in a low voice to Teddy as they walked behind the others to the East Room. She was trying desperately not to think of the two of them as a couple.

The headstrong look Teddy received from Quinn stayed his objection. He did wonder what had brought on her abrupt defensiveness. What was she flinging the gauntlet down about now?

They hung their coats up in the swank green-and-gold East Room. Allison was dressed similarly to Quinn, in a long apple-green wool skirt and a multi-colored sweater. Travis had on a gray flannel suit, a white button-down shirt and an uninspired maroon tie. Teddy hoped that jackets weren't required. He was wearing a dark blue sweater with his navy-blue slacks.

The maître d' seated them without comment, and Teddy breathed a sigh of relief. As did Travis. They were just barely in time to be offered the forty-five-dollar-a-head three-course prix-fixe meal.

A waiter hovered close by, not to intimidate, but as a reminder that they were just going to get in under the wire.

"I know what I'm having," Allison said, closing her menu.

Quinn leaned close to Teddy. "Don't be put off by the polenta crouton—the steak-and-mushroom ragout is excellent," she suggested.

Teddy gave her a droll nod. He knew she didn't intend to give him any grief with her concern, but it exasperated him. He wasn't a gourmet by any stretch of the imagination, but he didn't have any trouble reading a menu. He was a world traveler. Besides, polenta was Italian fare....

The waiter took their dinner choices, beginning with the women. With the exception of Teddy, each ordered the roasted corn soup with cilantro cream as a starter. Teddy requested a double salad.

Quinn, Allison and Mitchell selected a seafood trio with an inventive, French-sounding sauce. Travis went for the steak and mushroom ragout with the polenta crouton. Teddy opted for a fancy veal dish, though he would have preferred the steak.

The food arrived in record time.

"Have you seen the Picasso exhibit at the Museum of Modern Art?" Mitchell asked conversationally as their appetizers were cleared and their main dishes served.

"Yes," Quinn answered enthusiastically.

"Quinn and I went together last Saturday," Travis said.

Allison inserted, "I know I'm in the minority here, but I'd take a Degas dancer over a Picasso anytime."

Travis sent Allison a pinched glance. "Why do you always compare apples to oranges?"

Not at all put down, Allison laughed.

Mitchell eyed Teddy. "Are you into art?"

"I'm not much into the masters," Teddy answered coolly, trying to get with the program. "But I think today's sound is an art in itself."

Touché, Quinn thought, admiring the way Teddy handled himself. She couldn't imagine what had gotten into Mitchell.

Travis shifted to a new topic. "We still haven't gone skiing this season. Is anyone interested in going up to Vermont next weekend?"

"I can't make it," Quinn answered. She didn't think her gynecologist would approve of that kind of activity.

"Count me in," Allison said.

"I have to check my calendar," Mitchell responded.

Teddy kept slicing into his veal while Allison, Mitchell, Travis and Quinn debated the pros and cons of individual ski trails. There wasn't anything in the conversation that he could relate to. He thought about how many times he'd refused to go skiing with Quinn. Would it have killed him to learn the stupid sport?

Quinn glanced at Teddy without his notice. She remembered the time she'd talked him into going ice-skating with her in Central Park. They'd laughed over hot chocolates at Rumpelmayers and then gone back to the loft to massage each other's bruised bodies. It had been a good day.

A bell rang, reminding the diners that it was nearly time for the concert.

Mitchell summoned their waiter. "We'll pay now and have dessert during intermission."

Teddy didn't say a word when Quinn took her wallet out.

It took a few minutes to work out everyone's change, and then they walked back through the Carnegie Hall Museum, with its cases of music memorabilia, to the concert hall itself.

Teddy made what he hoped sounded like a significantly impressed noise when Quinn pointed out Toscanini's baton. He would have better appreciated looking at movie memorabilia at Planet Hollywood, just down the block.

The lights dimmed in the hall just seconds after they took their seats. Quinn was on Teddy's right. Allison was to his left.

Teddy made a righteous effort to open his soul as the music began, but his soul remained obstinate. His eyes kept drifting over to Quinn. He studied her dark golden head, which was bent forward thoughtfully. She sat transfixed, inaccessible to him.

Teddy mapped out some business strategy in his head to keep himself alert.

The intermission lights came on to the accompaniment of bravos and applause. There was a ruffling of programs amid buzzes of zeal and exuberance as the concert patrons stood, stretched, and marched toward libation. Champagne was being served in the lobby.

Teddy and Quinn headed with the rest of their party back to the East Room. They sat down at the same table and studied the dessert menu. Mitchell suggested they get a bottle of champagne. Teddy did a mental count of his funds while he glanced around, looking for credit card logos. He hadn't planned to be out for this kind of night on the town—Dutch treat or no Dutch treat.

"I don't care to have any champagne," Quinn said.

"I don't care for any, either." Allison shared a conspiratorial glance with Quinn.

The baby reminder revitalized Teddy. His mind awoke from the slow death he'd been putting it through. "I'm on the wagon myself," he said, drawing a snappy sneer from Mitchell.

Quinn's eyes met Teddy's, and she smiled. He smiled back at her. It was the kind of moment that memories were made of. It was the best moment he'd had since arriving at the concert hall.

Quinn and Allison each ordered a slice of pumpkin-apple pie and decaffeinated coffee. Mitchell settled for a Campari and soda with a wedge of Brie and crackers. Travis requested an espresso and a cranberry dumpling. Teddy elected to have coffee—just coffee.

"Did you want that decaffeinated, sir?" the waiter asked.

"No," Teddy answered. Thinking about listening to more Beethoven, he decided he'd drink it black.

For close to an hour, the three cups of unadulterated caffeine that Teddy had swallowed did the trick. Then tedium took over.

Teddy woke to the rousing applause that ended the concert. Blinking, Teddy's eyes met Quinn's in the illuminated auditorium. Her eyes were not the only eyes on him. The other three also had him dead to rights.

Teddy looked aside, trying to dodge the attention. "I don't know what happened to me," he said, frustrated. "I guess it was jet lag."

"Teddy just returned from Japan this evening," Quinn offered quickly.

Teddy felt as rotten as he knew how to feel, listening to Quinn trying to back him up. The excuse he'd given wasn't even in the neighborhood of the truth. He'd slept the entire flight from Japan.

Mitchell delivered a defense counsel's smirk to the four-member jury of his peers. Travis didn't have to be sold.

Allison sided with the defendant. "I've had jet lag that lasted for days."

"Weeks," Quinn added, giving Teddy's hand a fierce squeeze as they left the hall and walked back to

the East Room for their coats. She was still pleased
and touched that he'd come along to begin with. It
meant a lot to her, and she wanted him to know that.

Teddy returned only part of Quinn's touch. He was
busy beating himself up. Why couldn't he get himself
to be what she wanted?

It was nearly eleven-thirty when Quinn and Teddy
arrived back at Quinn's condo. They'd been quiet
during the ride.

"I'll make coffee," Quinn said, opening her apartment door.

Teddy hesitated at the entrance. "Maybe I should
just say good-night." He wasn't sure how much more
he could take of being around her and not touching.
He had his wayward hands pocketed in his leather
jacket.

"Just stay for a while." Quinn's voice was unsteady. She wasn't allowing herself to decide what she
wanted of him, only that she didn't want him to
leave. . . . Not yet.

"All right. One cup," Teddy conceded, willing
himself to test his powers of restraint as she raised inviting eyes.

Quinn flew to the kitchen.

Teddy closed the front door behind him and paced
around the living room.

"Aren't you going to take your jacket off?" Quinn
asked, coming back for him after having given him
time to follow her into the kitchen.

Teddy gave an inaudible sigh and shrugged his
jacket off. Quinn took it from him and hung it up in
the hall closet.

"The coffee should be ready," she said, all edgy, after they'd eyed each other for a few moments.

Teddy went with her as she took off for the kitchen. Quinn poured out two cups at the counter.

Teddy pulled out one of the two ladder-back chairs at the narrow bleached-oak table and sat down. The kitchen, done up in yellow and white, was small, neat and compact. He'd only been in the room once before, when he'd packed up her favorite dishes to move to the loft.

Quinn set a cup down in front of Teddy. The yellow sugar bowl that had once sat on his counter was on the table. She went to the refrigerator and poured milk into a matching yellow creamer. She brought it to the table, along with two white paper napkins that she folded and topped with yellow-handled stainless-steel teaspoons. He wondered if the silverware was new. Or had she forgotten it when he'd moved her out?

"Still no morning sickness?" he asked, fixing his coffee with milk and sugar after Quinn had prepared hers.

"Actually, I was a little queasy yesterday." Quinn kept stirring her coffee. She didn't really want to drink it.

"If you eat some saltines when you feel that way, it should help."

Quinn's eyes widened. "How do you know that?"

Teddy cast an uneasy glance her way. "I've been doing some reading."

"You have?" Quinn was stunned.

"Uh-huh." He wasn't sure he should be telling her. What if she felt he was carrying his involvement too far?

"I've thought of reading up myself, but I haven't got around to it." She looked down into the murky liquid in her coffee cup. She was elated by his concern. She just didn't know how to express her feelings. She wasn't very good at baring her soul.

Ill at ease, Teddy pressed the crease of one trouser leg between his fingers. "I'm pretty sure I've cornered the market. I'll bring you over some books."

"Thanks."

Their eyes met across the table. They both wanted to reach out and touch, but neither of them dared.

"Have you been back to the doctor?" He was talking to cover his jumpiness now.

"I have an appointment for next week."

"I'd like to go with you, if you wouldn't mind."

Quinn wasn't sure why, but she found the suggestion embarrassing. "I don't think that would be a good idea."

When she glanced at his face, Quinn was instantly dismayed at herself for discouraging him. She hadn't meant to get him disheartened.

Teddy drank some more of his coffee and put the cup down. He checked his watch. "It's getting late."

Quinn couldn't let him leave on this note. "Stay a little while longer." Her eyes pleaded with him. "I thought I could try on one of the kimonos."

Teddy ran an agitated hand through his hair. "All right." It had been a nerve-racking night for him. His constitution was taking even more punishment now that he was alone with her.

Quinn vaulted from her seat. "Bring your coffee into the living room," she called to him in midstride.

Teddy stayed where he was a few seconds longer—long enough to give himself a slow-motion right punch to his jaw. Get those sexy thoughts out of your head, he chastised himself.

Quinn put the pink kimono on over her sweater and skirt. Hurriedly, she checked her reflection in the full-length mirror hanging behind her closet door. She looked puffy, she realized, distressed. And her hair was a mess . . . and she needed some lipstick . . .

Rushing, she took the kimono off. She clambered out of her sweater and skirt. She yanked her boots off and put the kimono back on over her full slip. She tied the sash loose, then tighter, as she self-consciously dealt with the slight thickening of her waist.

She brushed her hair. She powdered her face. She reapplied lipstick—the pale umber tone that she favored. She lavished Obsession behind her ears and where her pulse was drumming a raucous beat at her throat. She didn't need any blush. Her face was all flushed.

Breathing rapidly, Quinn pulled open her bedroom door and walked into the living room. She nearly tripped over her own feet and had to right herself gracelessly. She was ever so thankful that he had his back to her and had missed her skid.

Teddy got up from the rattan couch. He had his jacket on. The sight of her in the pink silk, standing before him in her stockings, just about brought him to his knees. He jammed his hands into his pockets.

"Could you please say something?" Quinn fiddled haplessly with her sash. Her heart was doing somersaults as she tried to gauge his reaction.

He rewarded her with a low whistle.

"Satisfied?" he asked tightly.

Quinn rocked in place. His attitude came as a shock. "Why are you angry?"

Angry hardly covered it. Every nerve and muscle in his body was taut. "Let me ask you a question, Quinn. Are you trying to see how far you can go before I make a move?"

Quinn swallowed loudly, aggravated with herself and with him. "I guess we're having one of those double whammies you predicted," she conceded, because there didn't seem any way of getting away with a lie.

Teddy clicked his tongue on the roof of his dry mouth. "I guess so."

Quinn struggled for composure. "I don't think we should act on it." She felt like such a hypocrite, wanting him at the same time she was pushing him away.

Teddy dragged in a megabreath. He knew beyond a doubt that he could persuade her differently. He also knew beyond a doubt that not persuading her was best for both of them—at least at the moment.

"You don't have to panic, Quinn. I have a rule about trying not to foul up more than once a night. I figure I used up my allotment falling asleep at the concert."

Quinn lost her aggravation immediately. "It doesn't matter that you fell asleep." She didn't want him to put himself down.

"It matters." Teddy walked toward the front door. "It matters." He stepped out to the hall and closed the door behind him.

Chapter Five

"Are you sure that you don't mind this?" Teddy asked.

"Don't be silly," Quinn answered with faked calm. Her nerves were in knots.

The only wedge Teddy had been able to find to park his car in was a good walk from the restaurant. It was Saturday night, and Greenwich Village was hopping.

"I understand the food is very good," Teddy remarked as they strode briskly down Fourth Street.

Quinn thought she sensed some underlying vibrations in his voice. Was he tense? Or was her own tension increasing?

"Are you nervous?" She angled him a glance.

"I'm not nervous." Teddy manufactured a smile. It only made its way up one side of his mouth.

Quinn lifted a hand to catch her hair as the wind blew it in her face. "Do you think I'm dressed right?"

"Absolutely."

"Did you really notice what I'm wearing?" Now that she thought about it, he'd seemed distracted when he picked her up.

Teddy turned his eyes on Quinn and gave her a quick survey. Her closed black coat didn't give him a clue. However, the color blue came to mind.

"You're wearing a blue dress. Very pretty." Gripping her elbow, Teddy steered her around a group of punkish-looking teenage boys who were conversing loudly.

Quinn mentally grimaced. She wasn't dressed in blue. She was wearing a black-and-white houndstooth-check shirtdress that was buttoned up the front from the hem to her throat. She'd had to fight with the wide black patent-leather belt around her waist. She hadn't been able to hook it where it used to hook. It was now hooked three notches nearer to the end.

"Do you think that your sisters will be very dressed up?" She'd felt self-assured when she was dressing, sure that her outfit was correct—perfect for a dinner date.... Maybe she should have added jewelry.

"I've never paid attention to their clothes." Teddy halted their progress. He didn't have to be an Einstein to figure out that she was uptight—more uptight than usual. She did have a natural propensity for getting herself uptight.

"Quinn, if you want I'll find a phone and leave word at the restaurant that we can't make it."

"No." Quinn shook her head immediately. "I think it's wonderful that your brother and sisters want to take us out to celebrate our having a baby. Really..." She'd expected his family to want to be a part of their child's life. She just hadn't expected that they'd want to involve themselves with her.

Teddy searched Quinn's face as he stood bunched in his leather jacket with the collar turned up around his jaw.

"I want you to have a good time." He was getting himself all worked up, worrying that this night was going to be a bust. He was so worked up over it that he wouldn't mind putting it off. He wanted her to like his siblings.

"We never did get a chance to really know each other," Quinn said. Did they think she needed loosening up like her in-laws?

Former in-laws, Quinn reminded herself.

"Your sister Angie is the one married to a police officer, right?"

"Yes, Rick," Teddy answered.

They started walking again.

"I suppose she's had the baby by now."

Teddy nodded. "Three days before Christmas. She had another girl. Girls seem to run in the family." He had a strong feeling that they were going to have a boy—not that having a girl would bother him any. A picture of Quinn as a little girl came into Teddy's mind, and he smiled.

"What does Nancy's husband do?" Quinn was annoyed with herself for not remembering.

"Shep is a salesman for Lorene Fashions. Nancy met him when she was working as a secretary at the garment center. They got engaged three weeks after their first date, and were married six months later. Nancy and Shep had the record for short courtships in the family before you and me."

We also have the record for short marriages, Quinn thought unhappily.

"Here we are," Teddy said as they stood in front of Christopher's.

"Yes." Quinn made an attempt to smile and crossed her fingers. She would have been lying to herself if she'd tried to pretend that she didn't care whether or not his siblings liked her. Still, the absurdity of the situation wasn't lost on her. What possible difference did it make at this point? They were divorced, and that was that....

"Let's hit the beach," Teddy said, opening the front door.

Quinn unbuttoned her coat in the vestibule. Teddy helped her take it off.

"Are those blue-and-white checks?" he asked hopefully as his eyes worked over her.

Quinn smiled, naturally this time. "No. You must have been thinking about your blue shirt."

"How do you know what I'm wearing?" He grinned. "I haven't taken my jacket off."

"You had your jacket unzipped at my apartment. Dark blue shirt and splashy blue tie." The splash was a riot of orange and green over navy. Quinn thought there might even be a bit of gray. He had paired his shirt and tie with gray slacks.

Smiling, Teddy opened his jacket and shrugged it off. "I really did think you were wearing blue, but black-and-white is even better."

"At least I don't have you seeing red," Quinn quipped, astounding herself by bantering.

"What am I hearing? Are you turning glib on me?" There was a sizable dose of astonishment on his face.

"Well, you know what they say about people who spend a lot of time together...." She was enjoying herself with the novelty of having one-upped him for once. Repartee was more his department.

"You're letting me rub off on you, and you're still smiling." He teased her with his eyes. "What is this world coming to?"

Quinn put a fist to his upper arm and hit him lightly. "You'd better watch it. I might start rubbing off on you."

Teddy was bowled over. She was showing him a sense of humor. He hadn't been sure she had one. Who would have guessed?

"We have been spending a lot of time together," Teddy drawled comfortably. "It's fine with me. How is it with you?"

"Don't you think you should hang our coats up?" Quinn asked, evading the question.

Teddy grinned languidly. "I will after you answer my question." His gaze lowered to her mouth and lingered there.

Quinn glanced down at her feet. The look he was giving her was lethally seductive. "It's fine with me. Now, will you please stop being sexy?"

Teddy rolled his rascal eyes. "How do you like that? You're already rubbing off on me."

Quinn groaned comically. "You don't get your sexiness from me."

"You're wrong about that." Teddy smiled and found some hangers. What was the key here? Was he better off not noticing what she was wearing?

Frankie and Lisa, with their dates, were already waiting in the lounge. The bar divided the restaurant side of Christopher's from the club side.

Watching the doorway, Frankie spotted Teddy and Quinn as they stepped across the threshold. He waved them over.

Lisa quickly swung off her bar stool to give Quinn a big hug. "Johnny and I are back together," Lisa said in her ear.

"Great," Quinn whispered back, smiling at Teddy's youngest sister, who looked uninhibited and funky in a flouncy aqua minidress and lacy black leggings.

"Hi, Johnny." Teddy was staring daggers at Lisa's boyfriend. He didn't appreciate his sister being hurt.

Lisa pulled Johnny's arm. "Johnny, this is Quinn. Isn't she beautiful?"

"Yeah," grunted the broody-faced, dark-haired young man, who was dressed macho-sloppy in jeans, a white T-shirt and denim jacket.

Quinn was still blushing when Frankie introduced his date. "Teddy, Quinn, this is Kristen."

Kristen, who had been standing to the side, moved up next to Frankie.

"Kristen," Teddy said, giving the showy brunette's hand a shake.

"Hello," Quinn said, while her ego returned to reality. Kristen not only had a face to die for, but a body to match, too. The body was sheathed in a striking jade sweater-knit chemise that almost matched her eyes.

Colored contacts, Quinn decided, feeling catty. She wished her own hazel eyes were greener.

"Quinn, you look terrific," Frankie said, tipping forward to give Quinn a kiss on her cheek. "Can I order you a drink?"

"Speaking of drinks..." Teddy put an arm around Lisa. "What are you drinking, Peanut?"

Lisa wrinkled her nose. "Ginger ale. You don't think Frankie would get me a real drink, do you?"

"Just checking." Teddy grinned. "Quinn?"

"Ginger ale sounds good."

"Oh, there they are." Frankie picked out Nancy, Angie, Shep and Rick as they walked into the lounge. He put his hand up in the air to draw their notice. The lounge was crowded.

"Sorry we're late," Nancy apologized when they came over. "Hi, Quinn. Congratulations."

"Thank you." Quinn smiled, and then was assailed by a rotation of embraces, first from Nancy, then from Angie, Shep and Rick. Quinn was too overwhelmed by their lavishness to do more than just hang on. She worried that she was giving the impression of being uncompanionable and aloof. Frankie introduced Kristen. Everyone knew Lisa's boyfriend, Johnny.

"We'd better get into the restaurant before we lose our reservation," Shep said, looking very much like the odd man out, with his short stature and skinny frame.

"You packing your piece, Rick?" Frankie asked. "We may need it to get back our table."

With a snappy expression, Rick patted his black suit jacket under his left arm. He could have understudied for Sylvester Stallone. He had that kind of angular face. He had the build, and an aura of raw physical power.

Startled, Quinn stared apprehensively at Rick. They were just joking, weren't they?

"Rick is not carrying a gun," Teddy said in a quiet aside to Quinn as they made their way in a group through the lounge.

"I know that," Quinn replied, with an air of contrived insouciance. She felt foolish that she hadn't realized with certainty that the two men had been kidding.

"Quinn, come with me to the ladies' room?" Lisa asked as soon as they were seated in the dining room.

"That sounds like a good idea," Nancy decided.

"I may as well go, too," Angie said. "Kristen?"

"No, thanks," Kristen replied.

"Don't make it all night, ladies," Rick said as the four women got up from their seats.

"We won't," Angie returned, sending her husband a smile.

"I wanted to talk to Quinn alone," Lisa complained in the ladies' room.

"Let me guess," Nancy said as they all sat down on stools in front of a long horizontal mirror. "You want to ask Quinn what she thinks about Johnny."

Lisa pouted. "I already know what the two of you think." She looked in the mirror from Nancy to Angie.

"We just don't like the way he acts toward you," Angie said, seated between Nancy and Lisa. "He makes dates and breaks them. He says he's going to call and then he doesn't. Sometimes I feel like slapping you in the head."

Lisa laughed. "Okay...okay."

"I knew I needed to fix my makeup," Nancy moaned, peering closer at herself in the mirror. "The three of you are so lucky you're not old like me."

"Not that again." Angie grinned, bringing out the dimples in her cheeks. "You are only two years older than me, and I don't think I'm old just because I'm thirty. Besides, you have a figure. I look like I'm still pregnant." Angie fiddled with the shoulders of her ribbed tunic top, which was coordinated with her short, stretchy fuchsia skirt.

"You'll get your figure back." Nancy powdered her nose. "Next time I come over, I'm going to throw out any junk food I find."

Quinn, seated next to Lisa, glanced in the mirror at Angie, with her moppet's head of short reddish-brown hair, tangled in a bang on her forehead. Then Quinn glanced at Nancy, who had her darker brown hair tied back with a black velvet bow at the nape of her neck. Each of the sisters was vividly attractive, in Quinn's opinion. Before Quinn thought to be reserved, she offered, "You and Angie don't look any older than Lisa. I feel like a dowdy librarian next to the three of you."

Nancy closed her compact and got to her feet. "Stand up," she said, coming over to Quinn.

Quinn got to her feet. Angie and Lisa turned around on their stools.

"Open the buttons at your neck," Nancy instructed after a second of thoughtful evaluation.

Quinn undid the first two buttons.

"One more," Angie added. "And open some of the buttons on the bottom."

Quinn looked down at herself. "But my slip will show."

"Is it a half-slip?" Lisa asked.

Quinn nodded.

Lisa was quick to arrive at a solution. "Take it off."

"Good idea." Nancy agreed.

Quinn hesitated.

"Come on, Quinn," Nancy prompted. "We are not going to allow anyone in our family to feel dowdy."

Quinn thought to mention their lack of familial ties, then decided she didn't really want to. Instead, she pulled her slip down from under her dress. She folded it up small and stuffed it into her handbag. Then, bending over, she opened the last two buttons on her dress. Nancy bent over and opened one more.

"There," Nancy said, satisfied. "Now don't let me hear the word *dowdy* again."

"I think we should get back out there," Angie said.

"Are you sure I'm not too old for the dress I'm wearing?" Nancy asked. The dress in question was a short, pencil-slim black number with a scoop neck.

"We're sure," echoed three voices.

Teddy tracked Quinn's approach as the four women returned to the table. He might not have been observant earlier, but he was observing right now as his eyes focused on her legs, on exhibit in gunmetal hose and black patent pumps. My, oh, my... She was full of surprises tonight.

"Mercy," Teddy said—for Quinn's ears only— when she sat down next to him.

Quinn was heady with excitement at Teddy's approval. For a second, and only a second, Quinn did wonder what was happening to her stringent mode of demeanor.

The menu was continental, and everyone ordered with relish. There was lots of talk at the table—one conversation riding into the next conversation with hardly a pause in between. Quinn tried to chime in, but she kept finding herself one topic behind and in danger of getting whiplash as she turned her head rapidly from side to side. She knew there had to be a knack to this, but the knack escaped her.

Frankie said to Teddy, "Kristen wants to know if you'll give her an audition. She's a singer, and she's just starting out. She's looking for a promoter. I told her that you're on your way to making it big-time in the business."

Kristen offered Teddy a strikingly demure gaze from under incredibly long lashes. "I hope I'm not taking advantage of you." She knew how to use her satiny voice to her best advantage.

Quinn gulped down a mouthful of steak she'd only half chewed. She glanced at Teddy and then at Kristen. Did she really expect that he wouldn't start a new relationship at some point?

Oh, sure, now there was a pause....

"Put together a demo tape for me and I'll listen to it," Teddy answered. He reached into his back pocket, took out his wallet, found a business card and passed it along to Kristen.

"Are you sure?" Kristen asked, her voice even throatier.

"I insist," Teddy replied.

Quinn noted the particularly sexy smile Teddy added to his insistence. Though she was still hungry, Quinn didn't feel like eating the rest of her meal.

"What do you say we all go dancing next door?" Frankie asked after the table was wiped clean of empty coffee cups and dessert plates.

Lisa and Johnny were quick to agree. Sitting around eating and talking on a Saturday night was not their idea of a fun time.

Nancy squeezed Shep's forearm. "It's been ages since we've been out dancing. What do you think?"

"The kids are at your mother's for the night. We can stay out as late as you want."

Angie looked appealingly at Rick.

"It's fine with me," Rick responded.

"Honey, are you sure?" Angie questioned. "You're on duty tomorrow."

Rick flashed a smile. "I've got more stamina than both your brothers combined. I'm a lean, mean, trained machine."

Frankie countered, "Speaking on behalf of myself and my brother, how'd you like to put some money where your mouth is?"

"We don't have to stay," Teddy said privately to Quinn after the check was paid.

"We could for a while," Quinn offered. She could tell that Teddy wanted to stay.

She wasn't much of a dancer. The club was jammed. There were a number of unoccupied tables, but none were free, as was evidenced by the clutter of drinks and handbags. The dance floor was packed and rocking.

They all crowded up at the bar. It was only a second before Quinn found herself alone with Teddy. The others had moved quickly away to dance.

"Ginger ale?" Teddy asked, trying to catch the bartender's eye.

"Yes," Quinn answered absently, watching the dancers. Where did one learn those steps?

Teddy ordered two ginger ales.

Quinn took a sip of her soda after Teddy handed her the glass. Out of the corner of her eye, Quinn noted the way Teddy's head was bopping in rhythm to the music. If one could call the blaring synthesized beat music...

Quinn knew Teddy wanted to be out on the dance floor, doing whatever it was they were all doing out there. Feeling awkward and wooden, Quinn made an attempt to validate herself by shifting slightly from foot to foot. She tried to keep time to the music, though her head was beginning to throb.

Frankie and Kristen returned. Teddy said something in a low voice to Frankie. Agonizing, Quinn wondered if Teddy was asking his brother for permission to dance with Kristen. But Frankie and Kristen took off again, and Quinn was left wondering.

A moment later, the music changed to a slow tune.

"Care to dance?" Teddy asked.

"Well..." Quinn said faltering. But she didn't resist when he took hold of her hand.

Teddy navigated a path to the dance floor for them.

"Did you tell Frankie to ask them to play something slow?" Quinn questioned.

"Yes." Teddy smiled brilliantly. He turned her toward him with a little pressure at the small of her back.

"Dancing is good exercise for you." It was also a perfect opportunity for him, and he wasn't about to let a perfect opportunity go by unanswered.

Quinn made her arms stiff enough to keep plenty of air between them. She stood poised, ready for him to lead.

He studied her position for half a second. He got her message, but he decided to ignore it. He drew her in close.

Quinn pulled back, pressing a palm to Teddy's chest for leverage.

"Would you mind telling me why we are dancing this way?" he asked, holding her with a good foot between them.

Quinn looked up with woeful eyes. She didn't want to be dancing this way. "We are trying to stay out of trouble. That's why."

Teddy grinned. "How much trouble do you think we could get into on a dance floor?"

"Dancing close can be very suggestive." Quinn used her pupil-to-teacher voice.

"I understand the problem...." He danced her around, still giving her space. "This is not your scene. That's why you've got yourself all braced."

"You only think you understand me," Quinn returned aloofly. She didn't want to concede that she felt like a wooden Indian.

"I suppose you understand me better than I understand you," Teddy said, challengingly.

"I think I do."

"What do you understand?" He held her eyes as she looked up at him.

YOU COULD WIN THE

MILLION DOLLAR GRAND PRIZE

IN *Silhouette's*

BIGGEST SWEEPSTAKES EVER!

THE BIG WIN

6 GAME TICKETS INSIDE!

ENTER TODAY!

IT'S FUN! IT'S FREE!
AND IT COULD MAKE YOU A
MILLIONAIRE

If you've ever played scratch-off lottery tickets, you should be familiar with how our games work. On each of the first four tickets (numbered 1 to 4 in the upper right) there are Pink Metallic Strips to scratch off.

Using a coin, do just that—carefully scratch the PINK strips to reveal how much each ticket could be worth if it is a winning ticket. Tickets could be worth from $100.00 to $1,000,000.00 in lifetime money ($33,333.33 each year for 30 years).

Note, also, that each of your 4 tickets has a unique sweepstakes Lucky Number . . . and that's 4 chances for a **BIG WIN!**

FREE BOOKS!

At the same time you play your tickets to qualify for big prizes, you are invited to play ticket #5 to get brand-new Silhouette Romance™ novels. These books have a cover price of $2.75 each, but they are yours to keep absolutely free.

There's no catch. You're under no obligation to buy anything. We charge nothing—ZERO—for your first shipment. And you don't have to make any minimum number of purchases—not even one!

The fact is thousands of readers enjoy receiving books by mail from the Silhouette Reader Service™. They like the convenience of home delivery . . . they like getting the best new novels months before they're available in bookstores . . . and they love our discount prices!

We hope that after receiving your free books you'll want to remain a subscriber. But the choice is yours—to continue or cancel, anytime at all! So why not take us up on our invitation, with no risk of any kind. You'll be glad you did!

PLUS A FREE GIFT!

One more thing, when you accept the free book(s) on ticket #5, you are also entitled to play ticket #6, which is GOOD FOR A GREAT GIFT! Like the book(s), this gift is totally free and yours to keep as thanks for giving our Reader Service a try!

So scratch off the PINK STRIPS on all your BIG WIN tickets and send for everything today! You've got nothing to lose and everything to gain!

© 1991 HARLEQUIN ENTERPRISES LIMITED

Here are your BIG WIN Game Tickets potentially worth from $100.00 to $1,000,000.00 each. Scratch off the PINK METALLIC STRIP on each of your Sweepstakes tickets to see what you could win and mail your entry right away. (SEE OFFICIAL RULES IN BACK OF BOOK FOR DETAILS!)

This could be your lucky day—GOOD LUCK!

FOLD AND DETACH ALONG THIS DOTTED LINE—RETURN ALL GAME TICKETS INTACT.

TICKET 1

Scratch PINK METALLIC STRIP to reveal potential value of this ticket if it is a winning ticket. Return all game tickets intact.

LUCKY NUMBER

1L 610686

TICKET 2
Scratch PINK METALLIC STRIP to reveal potential value of this ticket if it is a winning ticket. Return all game tickets intact.

LUCKY NUMBER

4U 718283

TICKET 3

Scratch PINK METALLIC STRIP to reveal potential value of this ticket if it is a winning ticket. Return all game tickets intact.

LUCKY NUMBER

3M 598461

TICKET 4
Scratch PINK METALLIC STRIP to reveal potential value of this ticket if it is a winning ticket. Return all game tickets intact.

LUCKY NUMBER

9P 604134

TICKET 5

FREE BOOKS

We're giving away brand new books to selected individuals. Scratch PINK METALLIC STRIP for number of free books you will receive.

AUTHORIZATION CODE

130107-742

TICKET 6

FREE GIFT

We have an outstanding added gift for you if you are accepting our free books. Scratch PINK METALLIC STRIP to reveal gift.

AUTHORIZATION CODE

130107-742

YES! Enter my Lucky Numbers in THE BIG WIN Sweepstakes and when winners are selected, tell me if I've won any prize. If the PINK METALLIC STRIP is scratched off on ticket #5, I will also receive one or more FREE Silhouette Romance™ novels along with the FREE GIFT on ticket #6, as explained on the back and on the opposite page.

NAME _____ 215 CIS AH75 (U-SIL-R-06/93)

ADDRESS _____ APT. _____

CITY _____ STATE _____ ZIP CODE _____

Book offer limited to one per household and not valid to current Silhouette Romance subscribers. All orders subject to approval.

PRINTED IN U.S.A.   © 1991 HARLEQUIN ENTERPRISES LIMITED.

THE SILHOUETTE READER SERVICE™: HERE'S HOW IT WORKS

Accepting free books puts you under no obligation to buy anything. You may keep the books and gift and return the shipping statement marked "cancel." If you do not cancel, about a month later we will send you 6 additional novels, and bill you just $1.99 each plus 25¢ delivery and applicable sales tax, if any.* That's the complete price, and—compared to cover prices of $2.75 each—quite a bargain! You may cancel at any time, but if you choose to continue, every month we'll send you 6 more books, which you may either purchase at the discount price . . . or return at our expense and cancel your subscription.

* Terms and prices subject to change without notice. Sales tax applicable in N.Y.

ALTERNATE MEANS OF ENTRY: Print your name and address on a 3" x 5" piece of plain paper and send to: Million Dollar Sweepstakes, 3010 Walden Ave., P.O. Box 1867, Buffalo, NY 14269-1867. Limit: One entry per envelope.

BUSINESS REPLY MAIL
FIRST CLASS MAIL   PERMIT NO. 717   BUFFALO, NY

POSTAGE WILL BE PAID BY ADDRESSEE

SILHOUETTE READER SERVICE
3010 WALDEN AVE
PO BOX 1867
BUFFALO NY 14240-9952

NO POSTAGE
NECESSARY
IF MAILED
IN THE
UNITED STATES

"I understand that you think we should get married again, even though, intellectually, you know it won't work."

"Speak for yourself. I'm not that intellectual."

Quinn was on a mission of reason. "You wouldn't want to marry me again if I wasn't having our baby. You know that we're a heartache together. You're not letting yourself think beyond acting responsibly."

He was irritated. "You know what your problem is, Quinn? You think too much."

"You don't think enough," Quinn returned. "I'm trying to think us into a manageable relationship."

Teddy had a slim grasp on his cool. "Could you define *manageable* for me?"

"I want us to be friends." She knew she was saying all the right words. Why did she hate every one of them?

"You mean like pals...buddies?"

"Yes." Quinn nodded forlornly.

Teddy measured her with his eyes. "As I recall, you were pretty friendly last weekend, when you tried on one of the kimonos."

Quinn sighed sharply, pinned to the wall by his veracity. She should have expected that he'd throw that back at her. "I think we should be very proud of ourselves that we didn't allow a momentary lapse to get out of hand."

Teddy gave a dry laugh. "If you're divvying up credit, you owe me a larger share."

"Fine," Quinn responded, chafed.

"You're not sounding very friendly," he taunted.

Quinn planted her feet. She'd had it with him and this conversation. "I'd like to go home."

"That figures." He gave her an all-too-meaningful glance that Quinn had no trouble interpreting. Only she didn't feel that she was ducking out on his high-impact conversation. She was putting her manners to good use, avoiding an unnecessary confrontation.

They said their goodbyes, making their way around the dance floor. It didn't take long for Quinn to find herself standing stiffly in the restaurant's vestibule, with Teddy holding her coat open for her.

"Wait here. I'll get the car," Teddy said, zippering his jacket.

"I don't mind walking," Quinn replied formally.

"Stubborn," Teddy muttered, holding the door open.

"I heard that," Quinn retorted, passing by him with her nose turned up in the air.

They walked side by side with the wind in their faces, whipping through their hair. Teddy saw Quinn shiver as she crunched the front of her coat to her neck. He strung his arm around her shoulders, buffering her as best he could.

"Don't pull away." He used a voice that wasn't going to brook an argument.

Quinn didn't want to pull away. She was hoping she could find a way to end this evening on less of a sour note.

They strode the three blocks to the car without speaking.

Teddy held on to Quinn even as he bent to put the key in the passenger door. Staying tucked at his side, Quinn had to lean sideways with him as he opened the door.

When he turned her loose, Quinn slid into the bucket seat. Teddy closed the door and walked around the front of the car. Quinn watched him get comfortable at the wheel. He started the engine. He gave a touch to the rearview mirror and then, with his right hand on the floor shift, he drove the Corvette away from the curb.

Quinn's throat was dry. "I'm planning to go look at baby furniture and wallpaper next Saturday. Would you like to come with me?"

"Okay."

She wanted him to look her way, but he didn't. And he'd accused her of being stubborn...

Quinn drew in a full breath. "Do you want to talk about it?"

Teddy kept his eyes straight ahead. "I don't know anything about baby furniture."

"That isn't what I'm referring to."

"What are you referring to?"

"All right." Quinn bit her bottom lip. "I guess you don't want to talk about it."

He gave her a fast glance. "I'd talk about it if I knew what 'it' was."

"Forget it," Quinn said, crestfallen.

His eyes flicked her way and stayed there as she returned his gaze. "What a twosome we are." His tone was exasperated, but it had mellowed.

"Yes." Quinn nodded.

"Hey, buddy." He gave her one of his rakish grins.

"Hey, pal." Quinn smiled back, very happy that he wasn't still angry.

Chapter Six

"I'll have an English muffin," Quinn said, closing her menu. "I'd like peanut butter on one half, and egg salad on the other half. Spread the egg salad thin, but heap on the peanut butter. No, wait a minute... Maybe I'll have..." Quinn paused to think.

Amused, Teddy watched Quinn as she worked on making up her mind. He'd been eager to share even the nuances of her pregnancy, and now that he was, he absorbed them with growing enjoyment.

The waitress, a redheaded young girl with a freckled nose and spaces between her teeth, studied Quinn, nonplussed.

"I'll stick with the peanut butter and egg salad," Quinn decided, holding to her initial choice. "And I'll have a decaf."

"Do you want those halves put together?" the

waitress asked, unaware that she was wrinkling her
nose.

"Of course not," Quinn replied airily.

"I'll have a toasted corn muffin," Teddy said when
the redhead turned his way. "Decaf, and two glasses
of milk."

"You're drinking two glasses of milk?" Quinn
asked as the waitress bounced off.

"No." Teddy winked. "You're drinking one. I'm
going to keep you company."

Quinn mimed gagging with a finger on the tip of her
tongue. "I've decided that I've had it with milk."

"I don't like it much myself," Teddy rejoined, sup-
pressing a racking urge to reach across the table just to
touch her.

Quinn did like his demonstration of proportional
commitment, even though she didn't say so. "I've
come up with a few solutions to the milk problem. It's
a question of substitution. For example, yogurt re-
places a glass of milk, or lots of cream
cheese...though I am getting tired of yogurt and
cream cheese. I'm going to switch to cheddar and
Swiss next week. I wish I could drink malteds or
shakes, but there's all those calories. I've had all sorts
of cravings lately. This week I haven't been able to stop
eating those cheesy curly things that come in a bag like
potato chips. I hope they're made with real cheese."

Quinn's eyes connected with Teddy's as she finished giving him her take on the subject.

"I know the kind you mean." He held on to her
gaze. He had all sorts of cravings himself....

"Not the crunchy ones. I like the ones that almost
melt in your mouth."

She was a nut, and he was nuts about her, he thought to himself. "This is the deal. You drink your milk, and I'll get you a whole case of the ones you like."

"Don't tempt me." There were other, more pertinent implications in her response—ones that she was fighting hard not to give in to. There were times, like this moment, when he made it near to impossible for her to hold on to the knowledge that, personality-wise, they were world's apart.

Smiling, Teddy gave his own temptation a ride as his eyes traced the captivating lines of her face. He adored the puckered fullness of her bottom lip, the impudence of her slightly elevated eyebrows, her bright eyes, her delicate nose. She was royalty—a golden goddess created by the Fates to teach him lessons he hadn't known that he needed to learn—and to drive him up the wall and around the bend in the process.

Quinn played with her silverware, commanding herself to stop looking at him. "What are you thinking about?"

"Wallpaper, baby furniture, and when I'm going to see something of Junior in that belly of yours," Teddy teased.

"I've been worrying about that myself. But Dr. Wextler told me that some women don't show until their seventh or eighth month. I can see the change in my body when I undress."

This time Teddy didn't even try to repress himself. He gave her a look that was unmitigatedly sexy. He didn't say anything. He didn't have to. His message was crystal-clear.

Quinn ducked her head down. "I really opened the door to that one, didn't I?"

"You did," Teddy agreed. "And here I am trying to be on my best behavior."

"Right," Quinn said, with mock sarcasm. He was unmanageable, and she was all breathless and aroused by the message in his eyes. "Will you please stop giving me pornographic looks? You're breaking the rules."

Teddy grinned. "Were pornographic looks part of the original rules?"

"If they weren't, I'm making an amendment."

"Do I get a vote on that?"

"No." Quinn smiled impertinently.

"I'm going to have to call for a judge's ruling on this."

The waitress returned just then with their breakfasts.

Quinn chowed down as soon as they had both been served.

"Drink your milk," Teddy reminded her while she chewed on her egg-salad muffin and sipped coffee.

"I will when I get to my peanut butter," Quinn told him, her tone jokingly belligerent.

Teddy commented, "You seem very free and easy today. How come?"

"I'm looking forward to our shopping expedition." That was only part of it. She'd had her third dance lesson the night before, and if she had to say so herself, to herself, she was really coming along. Only she wasn't going to let him know until she was ready to show off. Given the fact that she was taking a crash

course, Quinn didn't expect her presentation to be too
far away.

Teddy chewed the last of his corn muffin. "Do you
have a list of the items we're going to need?"

"Yes." Quinn opened her handbag and showed him
the small notebook she'd brought with her.

"Good." He wasn't at all surprised by her prepar-
edness. "I'll just copy off of you."

"What do you mean?" Quinn blinked, baffled.

"We'll need two of everything. A setup for your
apartment and a setup for mine." He figured his setup
was the one they'd use permanently. He did have the
larger apartment, after all....

Quinn's hazel-green eyes widened. "You're not
thinking that we are going to be switching the baby
back and forth, are you?"

That was not the way she had it planned. She
planned that he'd come over to her place to see the
baby just about whenever he liked.

Teddy gathered from the emotion in her eyes that
he'd just, inadvertently, upset her apple cart. Rebel
that he was, he had nothing against using even an ir-
rational approach with her.

"You did agree that we would be equal parents?"

"Yes, but—"

Winging it, he interjected, "I'm not suggesting that
we switch the baby on a day-to-day basis, as your
mother put it. What I'm talking about is having the
baby with me at least one weekend out of every
month. We'll have to work out a schedule of holi-
days."

She'd thought, up until now, that she was entirely
and solely in charge. She wasn't, and she had no one

to blame but herself. She was the one who had brought up this inane equal-parenting plan to begin with.

"Fine," Quinn said curtly. She didn't like it, but she had to concede fair was fair.

Quinn drank a gulp of milk as she chewed peanut butter abstractedly. Two of everything, she was thinking. Of course they'd need two of everything.

Teddy broke into her gloomy musing. "Are you planning to keep the baby in your bedroom?"

Quinn stared at Teddy across the table. To keep his word, Teddy took a swig of his milk.

"I'm going to turn my dressing room into a nursery." Quinn tempered her tone, trying to cover her agitation.

"That's a tiny room, isn't it?"

"It's large enough for a baby." This time the belligerence in her voice was not a joking matter.

"Jot down for me that I'm going to need an intercom system. I'll want to hear the baby from my spare bedroom." He milked his advantage for whatever it was worth.

Quinn pictured his roomy spare bedroom. It was going to make a much better nursery than her dressing room.

"We don't have to make a note of it. I'll remember." Delving for a distraction, Quinn picked up her milk. She looked into the glass, realized it was empty and set it aside.

Teddy watched her push away the plate with her half-eaten English muffin. "Are you ready to go?"

"Yes, just as soon as you finish your milk," Quinn answered, looking to annoy him.

Teddy grinned. "The things I do for you," he said, and chug-a-lugged his glass of milk.

"You think you're so cute."

"I think you're cute, too." He did his best to work his smile on her, without success.

Quinn didn't lighten up until they walked into the wallpaper store just up the street from the luncheonette. Quinn's earlier happy mood imbued her, catching her unawares. She was going to be decorating for her baby, and she wasn't going to think about any other issue for now.

They stepped from a ceramic entry onto thick cocoa-colored carpeting.

"This place is really small," Teddy remarked, glancing at an arrangement of dark green easy chairs clustered around six small individual tables. In the rear, two saleswomen sat at one of the tables, going over order slips—laying them down as if they were playing two-handed solitaire.

"I love it." Quinn was all enthused. "Selecting wallpaper can be stressful. What they've done here is to provide a relaxed and comfortable atmosphere."

"How did you find this place?" Teddy inquired, unimpressed.

"A recommendation." She'd been told that they specialized in designer papers.

Yuppy heaven, Teddy decided as one of the saleswomen approached. He'd shopped for wallpaper a few years back, when he'd decided to paper his bedroom. He'd gone to a warehouse where rolls of papers were stacked on rows of open-ended steel shelves. They'd probably be able to find the same selection there that they would here—only here they'd pay twice as much. Atmosphere tended to be costly.

"I'm Ms. Duncan. Can I help?"

It was Teddy the saleswoman addressed. Teddy noted her well-ordered attire—a white blouse opened one button's worth, and a marbled black-and-gray suit. He suspected that if there was going to be a sales technique involved, it would be intimidation delivered with disdain.

Teddy gestured with his hand, deferring to Quinn.

"We're going to be papering a nursery." Quinn beamed.

They were ushered to a table and left to settle in. Ms. Duncan walked to one of the side walls, where there were sliding doors with chunky brass knobs. She opened one with the same reverence with which one might have attended to a bank vault.

Quinn finished unbuttoning her coat. She took it off and draped it on one of the extra easy chairs. Teddy did the same with his leather jacket. He'd already checked her out, but he checked again. His eyes ran over the generously full ecru shirt tucked into black slacks. His attention settled on the gold chain belt at her waist, and then just below. He'd been right the first time. She didn't show at all—not in her clothes, anyway.

Quinn smiled his way, sharing her anticipation with him. Teddy smiled back, half his mind on her body, the other half on the chore ahead. He felt out of place in jeans and his light blue band sweatshirt stenciled with Addiction—the name of a group he was promoting. He thought of putting his jacket back on, but the heat was on too high.

Ms. Duncan came back to their table with two hefty books. "We can order companion material to parallel most of our papers, and we do have a seamstress on staff for upholstery and window treatments. The trend among decorators today is to achieve a completed look... a sweeping blend."

Teddy gave a show of indifference while Ms. Duncan read the front of his sweatshirt.

Quinn pictured doing a bassinet in material that corresponded to the walls. There was even a small window in her dressing room. She could also do a rocker to match, though that would have to sit in her bedroom.

"I'm so glad you mentioned that." Quinn's eyes were lit with her excitement.

"Me too." Teddy sensed that he was expected to be grateful for having received privy information that sounded to him like a clever way of padding their bill.

"I'll leave you to our two most popular books." Ms. Duncan backed away, looking satisfied that she was leaving behind the reverberations of her savvy pitch.

Quinn slid one of the books to the far end of the table and opened the other one. She set the book so that they could look together. Quinn gave each page a thorough study. Her head was tilted down. Her Dutch-boy blond hair was tucked behind her ears. She was set to do business.

Teddy pushed up the sleeves of his sweatshirt, making himself comfortable for the long haul. It appeared to him that they were going to be here for quite a while.

It took Quinn over an hour to go through the two books. When she was finished, each book had at least six markers flagging the pages that were going to require a second study.

Teddy slid back his chair and stood. "I just want to stretch my legs," he said in response to Quinn's quizzical glance.

"Did you see anything you liked?" She'd looked to him several times to see if he wanted her to mark a page. He seemed to be going along with her suggestions. She guessed, at this point, that he was going to ask her to select for him.

"They're all nice, I suppose." He'd looked at all sorts of checks, stripes, florals, teddy bears, ducks and nursery-rhyme characters. Nothing he'd seen so far turned him on.

Quinn returned to her task. It was just as well that he was leaving the selections to her. She thought about the bright red-and-blue upholstered pieces he had in his living room. When she'd first seen his loft, she'd wondered if he was making an attempt to display patriotism. She'd shot down that premise when she noted the purple-and-green throw pillows scattered around. That room was hardly as jarring as his bedroom. The wallpaper he had in there was a psychedelic nightmare.

Teddy wasn't left to mosey aimlessly for long.

"Ms. Duncan is on the phone," said the second saleswoman, a younger version of the other, also in a white blouse and dark suit. "Can I help?"

"Do you have another book I could browse through?" He'd toyed with the idea of opening one of the sliders and helping himself. Only he bet self-service was frowned upon. He didn't want to embarrass Quinn by getting his hands slapped.

"Your wife looks like she's going to have a hard enough time narrowing down her selection as is." Ms. Elliott had glanced over at Quinn.

"We're not married," Teddy explained. "We're each going to do our own decorating."

"I see." From the expression on Ms. Elliott's face, she didn't see at all. "But you are doing a nursery together?"

Teddy tried to clear the woman's confusion. "We're each doing a nursery."

"Two nurseries?"

"Exactly." Teddy smiled. "One at my place, and one at her place."

"I see." She got it now. "What type of paper do you have in mind for your nursery?"

"I don't know. I won't know until I see it. It has to hit me."

"Perhaps something a little avant-garde."

"Perhaps." He wasn't sure how to relate to her reference point. If avant-garde meant less bland, he was for it.

Ms. Elliott worked open a slider with the same deference as her colleague. She tapped the tops of the books with manicured crimson nails as she studied binders.

"There should be some nursery papers in this one," she said, drawing out one of the books.

With the book in hand, Teddy started toward Quinn. Seeing that Quinn was beginning to look flustered, Teddy sat down at another table so as not to disturb her.

He flipped pages and finally found a use for some book markers.

A half hour later, Quinn leaned back in her seat. She exhaled a relieved sigh and smiled her pleasure. It hadn't been easy, but she finally had it—two absolutely perfect papers, one for her nursery and one for Teddy's.

"Teddy..." Quinn whispered, gesticulating with a crook of her pinky.

"I'll take his order, and you can take hers," Ms. Elliott said to Ms. Duncan.

"I believe they are both my customers," Ms. Duncan pointed out.

Ms. Elliott clearly took exception to that. "I disagree."

"You've decided?" Teddy smiled, putting his book on the table as he sat down next to Quinn.

"Yes." For a good ten minutes, Quinn waxed poetic over her two choices as she turned the pages of her book, showing one paper, then the other.

Teddy sat impatiently through her dissertation. He couldn't wait to show off his two finds. "I'm down to two myself."

"Are you ready to place your orders?" Ms. Duncan asked, with Ms. Elliott at her side.

Quinn had her eyes fixed on Teddy. "What do you mean, you have two?"

"I have two that I'm trying to decide between," Teddy responded to Quinn while Ms. Duncan and Ms. Elliott pulled up seats.

"What two?" Quinn asked, disappointed that he hadn't capitulated to her decorating sense.

With a dramatic flourish, Teddy opened his book to the first page he'd marked.

Reflexively Quinn's head snapped back as a circus motif on a bright lilac background whacked her in the eye.

Teddy gazed down over Quinn's shoulder. "It's all here. Lions and lion tamers, clowns, jugglers, elephants and bareback riders. It looks like there's even a trapeze—" he indicated an edge with his finger "—right where the paper is cut."

Quinn made herself keep looking as she took it in one small square at a time. This had to be the brassiest paper she'd ever seen.

Quinn ingested a groan. "Could I see the other paper you're thinking about?"

In his enthusiasm, Teddy didn't notice Quinn's dismay. The two saleswomen were more observant. Ms. Duncan and Ms. Elliott exchanged an I-think-we-have-a-problem-here look.

Teddy put his hand on the second marker and opened the book to the page. "Do you see why I'm having trouble deciding?"

Quinn forced herself to peer down. She put the tip of a finger to each of her eyes and viewed his second selection through a welcome blur in her vision. The paper was covered with carousels, gaudy, blazingly painted carousels with multicolored larger-than-life horses, each flaunting a glittery headdress.

"I think this one is more creative, don't you?" Teddy asked, communicating his energetic exultation.

"Ah..." Quinn did hear a sound come from her mouth.

"You know what this one says to me?" Teddy continued, getting a new kick out of the swatch.

Quinn was speechless. She wasn't even going to try to come up with an answer. However, she did think to correct herself. The first of his choices was not the brassiest paper she'd ever seen. He'd managed to top himself.

Teddy answered his own question. "This one says feel free to march to your own drummer."

"Hmm..." Quinn attempted to calm herself with a thoroughly deep breath. "That's an interesting interpretation."

"If I could make a suggestion—" Ms. Duncan began.

Quinn interrupted. "Teddy, could I speak to you for a second?"

Teddy turned in his seat to face Quinn squarely. He was smiling.

Quinn got to her feet and beckoned to Teddy to follow her with a yank of her head. She was not smiling.

"Are you planning to paper all the walls in the bedroom?" Quinn asked when they were standing off to the side.

"Sure, I want the kid to have something to look at no matter which way he turns his head."

"I believe that he or she will be staring straight up for a while." Quinn spoke with her best diction.

Teddy ran his fingers through his hair and came up with a brainstorm. "What if I paper the ceiling, too?"

"No...oh, no...no..." Quinn babbled. "Babies aren't supposed to look at a ceiling. They're supposed to look up at a mobile."

"You're right. I forgot about that."

Quinn started to breath again, almost normally.

"I'll get either a circus mobile or one with colored horses. Which one do you think will be easier to find?"

Quinn brought her hands up to the sides of her head and pressed in on her temples. "I don't know...."

"Do you have a headache?" Teddy was getting in tune with her body language.

"No." Quinn dropped her hands hopelessly.

"What did you want to talk to me about?" Now that he was giving her his observation, he was picking up all sorts of vibrations.

"Nothing. I've changed my mind." She was all out of subtlety. Quinn walked back to the table and plopped down in her seat. She just couldn't bring herself to overtly hurt his feelings.

Teddy followed after her. "Am I to understand that you don't like my papers?" he questioned coolly, sitting down.

"Would you like some more time alone?" Ms. Elliott asked, and was ignored.

Quinn felt her palms grow damp. "It's not a question of like...." She couldn't come up with anything that would be tactful.

"Don't patronize me, Quinn. Just tell me. Or throw up on me... or something."

Ms. Duncan eye-signaled Ms. Elliott. In silent agreement, both women edged back their seats and took deliberate steps to the rear of the store. They were not out of earshot. Quinn and Teddy weren't whispering.

Quinn recognized the stubborn jut of Teddy's jaw. "All right, I don't like your papers. They're both too busy. A nursery should be delicate."

"How about fun?" Teddy inquired drolly.

"Fun?" Quinn repeated, tight-lipped. "Are you suggesting that my nursery won't be fun?"

"What fun is the kid going to have with yellow and white checks."

"It's gingham, not checks!" Quinn spouted.

"Excuse me. Gingham," Teddy said flippantly.

Quinn flung him a combative look. "I'm leaning more toward the teddy-bear border, anyway. Do you have a problem with that one?"

"I don't have a problem with it. But by the time the kid is tall enough to notice it, he won't have teddy bears on his mind. He'll be old enough to ask for the keys to the car."

"Stop referring to our child as he. He could be a she!"

Teddy corrected himself. "He or she."

Quinn stared at him. "Your point is moot, anyway."

"Moot?" Teddy thought he was going to need a dictionary, but then she elaborated.

"The point is that I will have moved into a larger apartment by the time he or she is that tall. That's why your point is moot."

That was his plan exactly. Only he wasn't proposing that they wait for the kid to outgrow the nursery.

Quinn broke her stare to drum her fingers on the table. He was the only person she'd ever met who could get her so riled. She'd been born even-tempered.

"Perhaps you'd both like to do this another day?" Ms. Elliott came over to suggest at the pause in the fray.

"I'm ready to place my order," Quinn retorted stiffly.

"So am I," Teddy responded, back to his cool. If she'd given him an inch instead of acting pompous with her moot points, he would have tried to see her point of view. Why did they have to turn wallpaper into a bigger issue than it deserved to be?

"Let me write your order at the counter," Ms. Elliott urged Teddy, making a clear attempt to separate them.

Accepting that recommendation, Teddy followed Ms. Elliott to the counter. Ms. Duncan stepped over to Quinn.

In a huff, Quinn placed her order.

Ill-humored, Teddy placed his.

"It's a good thing those two aren't married," Ms. Duncan said to Ms. Elliott as Quinn and Teddy walked out the door.

"Which one did she pick?" Ms. Elliott asked.

Ms. Duncan opened the book for Ms. Elliott to see. "And he?"

Ms. Elliott passed her order pad to Ms. Duncan.

Quinn and Teddy marched toward Bloomingdale's. She strode at his side with her usual long-legged grace, but they couldn't have been farther apart if they'd been walking on opposite sides of the street. The freezing temperature in the air was nothing compared to the frigidity between them.

No way, Quinn decided, was she going to ask Teddy which paper he'd finally settled on.

As it turned out, she didn't have to ask. He gave her a broad enough clue when he selected a circus mobile after they'd each placed a layaway order for a white crib, a white bassinet, a white dressing table and a white carriage that could be turned into a stroller.

"Aren't you ordering a mobile?" Teddy asked passively.

Quinn's chin came up. "I'll come back and do it another day. I'm still deciding." She hadn't been able to find anything that would be frolicky enough against a background of gingham, and she was ticked off. She wouldn't have to be thinking frolicky if he wasn't doing fun....

Teddy spotted a pretzel vendor as they walked out of Bloomingdale's. "Would you like one?"

"All right," Quinn responded vaguely, envisioning circuses and carousels in her head. Was the baby going to prefer checks to looking at a circus?

Quinn sighed. Was she doing delicate, or dull?

Quinn ate three bites of her pretzel and then tossed it into a litter can as they retraced their steps on their way back to Teddy's car. She had things on her mind. She wasn't interested in eating.

Quinn stopped as they started to pass the wallpaper store. "I...ah...I've got to run in for a second."

"For what?" He'd had enough of wallpaper to last him for the rest of his life.

Quinn scoured her mind for a legitimate excuse. Finally, she came up with one that sounded plausible. "I...I don't think I gave my apartment number with my address."

Teddy yanked open the door.

Quinn nearly shoved him aside. "You don't have to come in with me."

"Fine." Teddy shrugged.

Ms. Duncan spotted Quinn as she entered. "Is there something more I can do for you?"

"Yes." Quinn breathed a smile. "Change my order to the other paper that Mr. Falco was looking at. The one with the carousels."

"We don't have material to match that one."

"That's okay."

Teddy was braced against a brick wall at the end of the store's window. He had just finished off his pretzel.

"All set?" he asked when she came up to him.

"Yes." Quinn couldn't meet his eyes. It was hard to admit being wrong.

Teddy reached for Quinn's hands and firmly drew her toward him, couching her in the spread of his legs. "Which paper did you pick? The gingham or the teddy bears?"

"Why?" Quinn's cheeks reddened, from inner heat, not outer chill.

Teddy cocked his head at her and smiled. "If you did the gingham, I'll change mine to the teddy bears."

"No. You can't." Quinn nearly laughed. "I changed my gingham to your carousels."

"You did?" He was astounded.

Quinn nodded, her face all flushed again. "Don't gloat. Okay?"

He clutched her around the neck, making her look at him. Then, heedless of passersby, he placed his mouth on hers as soon as he had her positioned.

"Teddy!" Quinn shrieked. "We're in the middle of a street."

Teddy grinned, releasing her. He did prefer this objection to some of the others she had. Though he did think to mention to her that she was a lot safer with him out in the open than she would have been indoors and alone.

Chapter Seven

The car had heated up, and Quinn sat relaxed, settled into the low black leather seat at Teddy's side. He was taking her home now that they'd finished shopping. Without conscious thought, Quinn set a nurturing palm on her stomach, slipping her slender hand between the buttons of her coat. It was a telling sign, and Teddy observed it.

"We should celebrate tonight." He smiled as she cut her eyes toward him. He ached to add his caress to her belly.

"What would we be celebrating?" Quinn kept her gaze leveled in his direction.

"Getting through the wallpaper crisis." He was thinking ahead, devising a new excuse to be around her, putting his inventiveness to work.

She was still a little in shock that she'd conceded to his line of reasoning over the wallpaper without feeling at all compromised. And she was further shocked thinking about his willingness, in the end, to compromise with her. This was a first for them. It would have been more in keeping with their past behavior had they stubbornly held their positions and refused to give way. This getting along was a curious experience. Quinn wasn't quite certain how to examine it.

"We can celebrate tonight with dinner," she suggested, agreeing. "We'll go Dutch treat." She wasn't about to let herself get overly excited. One crisis resolved didn't make for a compatible relationship—not even an unmarried compatible relationship.

The Dutch-treat business, once again, he thought, chafing, but he let it pass. He wasn't going to deliberately start a discussion that might evolve into an argument. He was certain that there were more than enough arguments somewhere out there, lined up, waiting for them to stumble over.

"Where would you like to go? I'll call and make a reservation when we get to your place."

"Let me think about it." At the periphery of her vision, Quinn noted the pull of faded Levi's denim over the prominent muscles of his thighs. She glanced at his scuffed western boots, which were licked over with a natural polish. No doubt he'd change to slacks and a shirt, perhaps even a suit, depending on her choice of restaurants. He did own a number of suits—not that there was a conservative or traditional one in the bunch. The few times she'd requested that he dress up, he'd favored a double-breasted suit that he teamed with a sharp blue shirt and a print tie. And he'd wear his London Fog trenchcoat against the chill. For some reason that she couldn't pin down, Quinn decided she didn't want him to change out of his jeans and his Addiction sweatshirt, which should have embarrassed her, but hadn't, when she first noticed it in the wallpaper store. Was it possible that she was becoming a little less reserved?

Teddy kept quiet, letting Quinn think, and he thought himself. He thought about her in the morning, padding around his loft in heavy athletic socks scrunched around her ankles and a man-tailored nightshirt that only just concealed her bikini panties. The weekends had been the best when he was in town and she didn't have a class to rush to—when he could teasingly manhandle her into an a.m. demonstration of the passion they both felt. It had to be a contradiction of the laws of human nature for that same passion to be getting in his way now. But it was in his way. He knew he had to prove to her that there was more than sexuality between them—not that he intended on letting her forget that part of it.

Teddy forced his meandering thoughts away from dangerous territory. The fly of his jeans was already uncomfortably tight.

"Let's have pizza tonight," Quinn said.

"Pizza?" Teddy appraised Quinn's expression as long as he could and still drive safely. "Since when do you like pizza?"

"It's not me," Quinn responded lightly. "It's the baby. The baby wants pizza." She hoped that he realized that she was trying her best to be accommodating.

"In that case..." Teddy smiled at her as his voice drifted off.

"Teddy?"

"Yes." He heard a serious note in her tone now, and when he checked her face he saw that her eyes were solemn.

"Do you know anything about taking care of a baby?"

He meditated on her question for a second before answering, "Not really."

"I'm terrified," Quinn confessed, revealing some of her vulnerability.

Knowing her as he did, he knew she was probably obsessing. "I'm sure we'll learn as we go along, the way everyone else does."

"There's always Dr. Spock," Quinn reasoned, but she didn't brighten a whole lot. She pictured herself holding the baby in one hand and the book in the other. She wanted to be perfect, and confident.

Teddy empathized personally. "Too bad there isn't a place to go for lessons." She had *him* obsessing now.

Quinn nodded her head. "There should be a school for parents-to-be. Only I guess they'd have to do it with dolls, and that wouldn't be like the real thing."

"Wait a minute!" Teddy flashed her a knockout grin. "I know where we can go for lessons."

"Where?" Quinn raised a suspicious eyebrow. She didn't expect to concur with his idea—not when it came this spontaneously.

"You'll see." He was looking for a way to make a U-turn.

"Tell me," Quinn insisted cautiously.

"We'll go practice on my new niece."

"Angie's baby?"

"Yes." Teddy nodded. He had to be on a winning streak—first the wallpaper, and now a solution to her latest dilemma. Quinn Barnett might just as well throw in her hand right now, Teddy concluded, riding high.

Quinn was dubious. "You don't think she'll mind?"

"Angie?" Teddy shook his head. "She'll be thrilled that we're coming over."

"Wait a minute." Quinn raised her hand in a stop gesture. "You're not planning for us to just walk in on her?"

He answered without thinking. "My family doesn't stand on ceremony."

Quinn gave him a tight look before she decided that he wasn't casting aspersions on *her* family. However, she was not going to be diverted from her stand. "I'm not going unless you call her first."

"It's not really necessary."

Quinn stood her ground. Her manners were at stake. "If you don't call, I won't go."

"Okay, Quinn." He gave in to placate her. "Watch for a pay phone."

Two blocks later, Quinn spotted an outdoor booth. Teddy pulled over and double-parked.

"I'll be right back," he said, getting out of the car. "Don't worry. I won't push." He added the last, knowing she was about to consider that as a possibility.

Quinn admitted to herself while she waited that Teddy's idea, surprisingly, made sense. They were really working together—the two of them. They were becoming pals...buddies. She hadn't actually believed it would happen and certainly not this soon. She was thrilled...really thrilled....

Quinn leaned back contentedly in her seat.

Teddy smiled, getting into the car again. "She said yes."

Quinn straightened up. "She wasn't in the middle of anything?"

"No." Teddy started to drive. "They're going to wait lunch for us."

"They?" Quinn queried alertly.

"Nancy is over with the twins, and my mother and my Aunt Ingie are there. Angie is putting together some salads."

Quinn's serenity fizzled. "Oh, no," she muttered. "Did you tell Angie why we were coming?"

Teddy centered a glance on her. "Of course. That was the reason you wanted me to call, wasn't it?"

"Yes, but not if your mother and your aunt were there."

"What difference does that make?"

Quinn looked out her side window, expelled an aggravated breath and looked back at him. "You don't see the difference? Honestly, Teddy!"

"No, I don't see the difference. Honestly, Quinn!" he said, copying her tone of annoyance.

"Pull over," she said helplessly. How could she have thought it was okay to follow one of his impulses? She should have known that, given his way, he'd make her life utterly nerve-racking.

"What?" Teddy looked at her, unable to fathom her instruction, let alone her attitude.

"I'm not going empty handed. We just passed a grocery store." She might never change his family's opinion of her as rigid, but she could, at least, show them that she knew how to arrive as a guest.

He could think of thriftier places to shop than on Park Avenue. "I'll find a place to park."

Quinn waved away his offer. "It will take too much time. We're already holding them up."

"All right." He gave in to keep what was left of the peace. Pulling over, he double-parked again.

As soon as he had his foot on the brake, Quinn shot out the door.

She returned eight minutes later with a large shopping bag. She set it carefully on the floor in the back of the car, behind her seat.

Teddy muscled the Corvette back into traffic. "Will you please tell me now what you're upset about?" He'd tried puzzling out where he'd gone wrong. He still hadn't figured it out.

"You should have realized that I don't want your mother knowing I'm inept. I don't mind being inept in front of Angie, even Nancy, but your mother and your aunt..."

Teddy made the mistake of chuckling.

"There is nothing funny about this," Quinn spouted indignantly. "Your mother already thinks I'm stiff as a board. Now she's going to know I'm also incompetent."

Teddy adjusted his expression, trying to keep his amusement to himself. "Why don't you consider the possibility that you might not be incompetent? How hard can it be to learn how to take care of a baby?"

"It's easy for you to say. You're not the one who is going to be judged. How would you like it if my mother were there scoring you?"

"Just your mother? Or would your father be there, as well?" He was teasing her now.

"Well, since your aunt is there, then my father would be there, too." Quinn wondered in exasperation how he had managed to get her talking like a twelve-year-old.

"I do want to be fair." He favored her with a kidding glance. "I'm willing to pick your mother and father up. Then we can line them all up like an Olympic committee."

The image his joking conjured up forced a smile from Quinn. "My guess is that between us we couldn't pull better than a minus two."

Teddy laughed. "Are you sure you're not being too generous?"

Quinn's smile lingered. "Do you really have an aunt Ingie?"

"Uh-huh, but that's not her real name. I have no idea what her real name is. She's always been Aunt Ingie."

"What about Rick, Shep and your father?" She hadn't thought before about them being there.

"Rick, Shep and my father are working today. Is that better?" He'd heard the alarm return to her voice.

"Is there an Uncle Ingie?"

"There's an Uncle Bruno. . . ." Teddy paused intentionally. "He's not there."

"This is going to be so humiliating." Quinn raised her hands and covered her face.

Teddy reached out and gave her knee what he intended to be a comforting squeeze, but then he couldn't seem to pull his hand away.

Quinn's heart skipped a beat, rebounded and raced while she tried her level best not to feel any sort of sensation. Much to her emotional chagrin, Quinn

concluded, she'd indulged herself incorrectly. She did
not have the buddy system down pat. "Your hand,"
she said, slowly lowering hers from her face.

Teddy dragged his straying hand off her and onto
the wheel. "Sorry," he said, pitching her a whammy
of a look.

"Yes, I can see how sorry you are." Before she
averted her eyes, Quinn meet Teddy's with a look that
she hoped came off as detached.

Teddy wasn't deterred. "If you're going to make
that much out of it, I'm going to get ideas."

"I am not making anything out of it," Quinn retorted, the back of her head to his face. She was not
going to encourage his rowdy insinuation by acting as
his straight man. However, there wasn't much she
could do about the sensuous heat she was feeling inside.

To Quinn's considerable relief, Teddy dropped the
topic. In fact, he didn't say another word for the rest
of the ride.

"Are you sure you bought enough?" he quipped
later, carrying the full shopping bag up the walk to
Angie and Rick's garden apartment in Riverdale.

"Why did you buy so much?" Connie Falco asked,
overwhelmed, as she helped Quinn and Teddy un-
pack covered opaque containers, a tin of imported
crackers and a cake box in the kitchen.

Aunt Ingie popped one of the lids. "What is this?"
she sniffed.

Quinn took a look and smiled. "Pâté."

Aunt Ingie studied it warily. "What do they make
that from?"

"Don't worry about it, Aunt Ingie," Teddy chimed in. "It's delicious."

"Connie, did you ever have pâté?" Ingie questioned, pursing her mouth.

"No." Connie shook her head, glanced at Quinn's suddenly wilted presence and said, "But I've wanted to try it."

"Aunt Ingie," Angie called out from the dining room, where she and Nancy were setting out the fixings that had already been prepared. "Could you bring in a bottle of soda from the refrigerator, and the milk for the kids?"

"We are going to have some feast." Connie spoke cheerfully to Quinn as Ingie walked her generous frame out of the kitchen with the milk and soda.

Teddy gave his mother a grateful smile, and then cautiously cast his eyes on Quinn. He wished he'd gone into the grocery store with her.

Quinn was cognizant that Teddy was looking her way. She studied the table. She'd wanted to impress everyone with her choice of fine food. What she'd managed, instead, was to fall flat on her face. Why couldn't she ever get it right where his family was concerned?

Connie finished opening the containers. "Oh, lobster salad. Everyone loves lobster salad. And two desserts..."

"One dessert," Teddy said, checking, while Quinn stood stiff at his side. "That's not Jell-O, Mom. That's tomato aspic."

"But this is a cake?" Connie looked to her son for verification after raising the lid of the box.

"Almond torte," Quinn informed her, finding it hard to make her lips work. They felt starched.

"And this one?" Connie asked hesitantly, putting her hand on another container.

Teddy, glancing over Quinn's shoulder, decided not to venture a guess.

Quinn cleared a frog from her throat. "Smoked salmon with truffles."

Connie bustled. "Teddy, help me get down some big bowls, and a plate for the cake. Quinn, there should be a cake cutter and large spoons in that drawer." She pointed for Quinn's benefit.

They worked together emptying containers.

"Where does Angie keep her garbage?" Quinn asked in a strained voice, aware of, but refusing to meet the boosting looks Teddy kept sending her way. She'd selected the wrong foods. She knew it now, and she didn't want to be consoled. She was intent on toughing it out all alone. It was the way she operated. She'd honed that style growing up an only child.

"We'll save the containers. I have a feeling there'll be leftovers," Connie answered innocently.

Angie pushed open the swinging door. "Is everything ready to bring out?"

They all carried something into the dining room.

"I want the Jell-O," Kim protested to her mother as Nancy served her tuna-and-tortellini salad.

"Me too," said Stephie.

"I want me too," parroted Melissa, Angie's two-year-old daughter. She was in her high chair, kicking her feet under the table.

"It's not Jell-O," Connie crooned to the adorable, chubby two-year-old.

"It's not?" Nancy showed surprise.

"Tomato aspic," Teddy and Quinn answered at the same time.

Connie, having taken a seat next to Melissa, asked, "Angie, what do you want her to eat?"

"Do you put the pâté on a cracker or a plate?" Aunt Ingie asked.

"Try it on a cracker," Teddy suggested.

Angie handed her mother a jar of peanut butter, a jar of grape jam and two slices of white bread. "Put peanut butter on one slice, and jelly on the other. Don't put them together. She likes to eat them separately. Spread the jelly thin. She'll get it all over her."

"I want Jell-O," Melissa whined.

Angie let out a sigh. "Melissa, stop kicking or I'm going to pull your chair away from the table."

"I want big-girl chair," Melissa squealed.

Connie put the jelly half of the open-face sandwich she was preparing on Melissa's tray. "Eat your big-girl lunch."

Melissa continued to kick.

The adults began passing food around the table, serving themselves. Teddy heaped his plate with pâté, smoked salmon and tomato aspic, though his mouth watered for the antipasto and the tuna with tortellini.

Quinn, emoting her manners, did the opposite of Teddy. She took tiny helpings of the wonderful food she'd brought, favoring instead the food Angie had prepared. She was not particularly fond of Italian seasonings, especially garlic.

"If you throw it," Angie warned, watching Melissa wave her jelly bread, "you are not getting another one."

Melissa took aim with her pudgy little hand and tossed. It landed jelly-side-down on top of Teddy's tomato aspic.

Angie jumped up. Melissa giggled nervously. The twins laughed.

Nancy smiled at Teddy and Quinn. "See what you've got to look forward to?"

"Is that the baby?" Connie raised her hands to call for quiet.

Angie sighed raggedly. "It's the baby."

"Quinn and I will go get her," Teddy volunteered.

"You can't just bring her in." Angie turned to her brother. "She's probably wet."

"We'll change her." Teddy grabbed Quinn's hand and tugged her to her feet.

Angie looked from Quinn to Teddy. "She may be more than wet."

That possibility stopped Teddy short. He glanced indecisively at Quinn.

Connie Falco intervened. "Angie, fix your brother another plate. I'll help them with the baby."

Connie led the way, with Quinn and Teddy in tow. Teddy checked Quinn to see how she was taking his mother's well-meaning interference. Quinn rolled her eyes toward the ceiling.

The baby was fussing up a storm in the crib, and her vigor seemed to be increasing. She was wailing, and her tiny hands were tightened into fists.

"She's got some pair of lungs," Teddy said in amazement.

Connie smiled. "They all do. You especially, as I recall."

Quinn was getting anxious over the baby's crying.
"Should I lift her up?"

Teddy, bent on sparing Quinn any discomfort in
front of his mother, advanced. "Let me have first
crack at this."

Connie moved with Teddy. "Sh, sh, Lindsey. Nana
is here."

Teddy put his hands down into the crib, then re-
treated. "Boy, is she wet!"

"Do you want me to pick her up?" Connie asked.

Teddy was not going to back down in front of
Quinn. Inhaling, he took the plunge, placing his hands
under Lindsey's armpits. He lifted, holding her
straight up and away from him. Her pink jumpsuit
was wet all the way up the front, practically to her
neck.

Lindsey halted her screeching for a second, then got
her second wind and resumed. Teddy walked cautiously, carrying her like a sack of potatoes. He swung
her back and forth over the dressing table, trying to
find the right angle to set her down. "Help me out,
Lindsey," Teddy begged.

Lindsey squalled all the louder.

Connie prodded Teddy. "Just lay her down."

Teddy tossed his mother a groaning look. "I'm
trying to get her uncurled."

Instinctively Quinn reached out and took hold of
the baby. Lindsey raised her reddened little face, wet-
eyed. She'd found herself a mother, and she quieted,
though she still had her bottom lip stuck out. With her
breath caught in her throat, Quinn gently laid Lindsey down on the table.

Teddy ran a finger across the sweat that had collected on his brow before he fastened his eyes on Quinn. She was keeping the baby gentled with one hand, while her other hand was busy with snaps. Impressed, he watched her displaying an unfamiliar but innate knowledge of mothering, making the baby feel more secure than he knew she felt.

Her breathing not yet even, Quinn directed herself to Connie Falco for further tutelage while Lindsey lay complacently nude. The baby's jumpsuit was to one side, topped by a very wet disposable diaper.

"You did that so well...." Connie enthused, and Quinn was enraptured by her former mother-in-law's compliment.

"Now, you check." Connie grasped the baby's two legs with one hand. She raised her up, and they both inspected—though Quinn was not certain what she was looking for.

"Diaper rash," Connie pronounced, relinquishing her hold on the baby. "Use the cloth on her bottom, and then grease her up with some Vaseline."

Leaving Quinn to the task, Connie rid the table of both diaper and jumpsuit after ascertaining which were the appropriate covered pails beside the table.

Teddy's heart was near to brimming over with tenderness and pride for Quinn, and yet he felt left out. The more he observed Quinn, the more he felt left out, and threatened. She had it all together without any help from him.

"I don't see any Vaseline." Quinn glanced over her shoulder and saw Teddy. "Come here." She beckoned him closer with a tilt of her head, wanting him involved in her exhilaration.

Teddy smiled then. It was a big, relieved, wonderful smile now that he'd slain his dragons. Quinn blushed, because his mother was there and the look between them was private.

"I'll go ask Angie where she keeps the Vaseline." A little embarrassed, Connie made a fast exit.

Quinn and Teddy stood together, each with a hand on the baby. "You know what, Teddy?" Quinn murmured. "Maybe I'm jumping the gun, but I really think I'm going to make a terrific mother."

Teddy winked. "I don't think you're jumping the gun." She had him jumping through hoops.

"You're going to make a terrific father." Giving in to a flash of spontaneity, Quinn put a hand on Teddy's jaw and pulled his mouth to her lips.

Angie and Connie walked in just then.

"Kissing isn't allowed when you're tending to my baby," Angie kidded her brother.

"We're giving her a lesson on relating," Teddy joshed.

Connie had other fish to fry. "Teddy, move over so I can show Angie the baby's diaper rash."

"Oh, Mother, all babies get diaper rash occasionally." Angie moved up to the table, and Quinn stepped aside.

"She wouldn't get diaper rash if you used Vaseline on her," Connie responded resolutely.

Angie reached for a can from the shelf under the dressing table. "I've always used this medicated powder, and I'm happy with the way it works. I use it on Melissa, too." Angie began to sprinkle Lindsey's bottom.

Connie had a comeback. "Old remedies work best. But don't believe me. Ask your sister. I remember when she came crying to me that the twins had diaper rash, and I showed her how to coat them with Vaseline and cornstarch."

Angie fastened a diaper on Lindsey. "Mother, Nancy told me to use this powder."

Teddy brought his smile to Quinn's ear. "Shall we go eat while they duke it out?"

"Nancy, could you come in here?" Angie yelled.

Quinn and Teddy headed out the door.

"What time is it now?" Quinn asked, reclining alongside Teddy on the plump cushions of her rattan couch. She was too languid to lift her hand.

Teddy checked his watch. "Almost nine-thirty."

"Do you want some coffee?"

"No." Teddy turned his head to smile at her. "I'll go make some for you, if you want."

Quinn shook her head. "That pizza was good."

They'd picked up a pie after leaving Angie and Rick's apartment. They'd gorged themselves on it.

Quinn raised her eyebrow playfully. "I didn't think you'd be able to eat."

"What do you mean?" Teddy asked, feeling guilty. He hadn't thought she'd noticed the amount of tortellini salad he'd wolfed down when he'd gotten a second shot at lunch. Since she had paid attention, she must also have noticed that he hadn't eaten any smoked salmon or tomato aspic.

But Quinn was on a different path. "You looked positively green around the gills when Rick asked if we wanted to see the videos of Angie's two deliveries. I hope you're not going to be the type of male who faints in the delivery room...."

"Give me a break...." Teddy grinned. "Sicilian men are stallions. They don't faint. It's a known fact. I was just reacting to the whiplash my mother and Aunt Ingie had been giving my sisters all day."

Quinn didn't let him off the hook. "Your mother and your aunt had left hours before then."

"All right...I'm only half-Sicilian. My mother's family came from Napoli. I'm allowed a little leeway."

"What do you think about natural childbirth?"

Teddy rested his eyes watchfully on Quinn. "What do you think about it?"

Quinn pulled her lower lip between her teeth. "I like the idea."

Teddy straightened up. "I'd rather you be knocked out."

Quinn's fingertips touched Teddy's fingertips. "Natural is better for the baby. Will you take Lamaze classes with me?"

"Yes." He gave her the answer she wanted, but it made him crazy to think about her in pain. "Will you promise me that if it gets too rough you'll let the doctor give you something?"

"Yes." She appeased him, though she was certain that she wasn't going to chicken out. "Do you think we should use medicated powder or Vaseline?"

"I haven't decided that one." Teddy made himself smile so as not to betray the anxiety he continued to experience over the thought of natural childbirth. "I'm still debating whether to burp midway through a bottle or wait to the end."

"To burp or not to burp..." Quinn laughed, then quieted as her eyes were drawn to his.

They sat there intoxicated with each other. The air between them grew heavy with the suppressed feelings they'd both been living with for the past few months. Teddy told himself to get up and go home. He was on shaky ground—very shaky ground.

"Please don't let it go too far," Quinn whispered tremulously, knowing that if she didn't have something of him she was going to cry.

Baring his clenched teeth, Teddy groaned, then swore lavishly. "I promise, I promi—"

Quinn ended his words as she pulled him down.

They kissed, hot against each other, and while they did he changed their positions so that she sat on his lap. He raggedly murmured her name, struggling with his endurance to leave each move to her.

She threaded her fingers in his hair, directing him to her neck. Dragging her up higher, he nuzzled every inch, dropping a kiss on the lobe of each ear, tasting her perfume. He freed one hand to get to the buttons of her blouse. Making a low, hungry sound deep in his throat, Teddy sealed her mouth to his for a wildly, ravenous kiss.

Quinn quested as Teddy quested, and her mission was accomplished faster than his as she rode her hands up beneath his sweatshirt to cling to his bare back.

Her breasts were fuller than he remembered, and he drew back to see her with her blouse opened, discovering with his eyes while his hands cradled the silk and lace of her bra.

The phone rang, startling them both. Teddy froze. Quinn gasped.

"Don't..." Teddy pleaded, but Quinn was already pushing away, taking her hands from him to bunch her blouse closed with a tight fist.

Flushed and unsteady, Quinn hobbled across the room to pick up the extension in her bedroom. She didn't bother to close the door.

Teddy fell back against the couch, strung out. He heard Quinn say, "Hello," and listened inertly to her end of the conversation. He could tell that she was speaking to her mother.

"My mother and father have extended us both an invitation," Quinn said when she returned, her blouse buttoned and tucked back into her slacks. "I think they're becoming jealous of the time we've been spending with your family."

"What kind of invitation?" he asked, watching her look everywhere but directly at him.

"A dinner party." Quinn stared at her feet. She was still very aroused. "Next Saturday. Will you go with me?"

"Sure," Teddy answered in a tense voice, pained by her body language and by his lack of control. "Do you want me to leave?"

Quinn closed her eyes for a second, then nodded her head.

Teddy yanked himself up from the couch.

Quinn walked him to the door.

"Good night, Quinn." He wasn't seeing more than the side of her face.

"Good night, Teddy." Quinn stepped backward so that he could open the door.

Chapter Eight

Teddy did a double take. "Do I have the wrong night?" His bewildered gaze traveled over Quinn. She wasn't dressed the way he'd expected her to be dressed, especially to go to her parents.

Quinn laughed. "We *are* going to my parents. Tonight is their dinner party." Quinn swished provocatively, intentionally causing a bounce to her short—almost mini—sleeveless red swing dress. She didn't look at all pregnant. The generous flare of the moiré-and-crepe dress nicely concealed the growing roundness of her belly.

Teddy ran his appreciative gaze over Quinn a third time. He dropped his eyes to her black suede pumps. He raised them slowly to her gorgeous legs—all tease in sheer black hose—to the evident lushness of her breasts, and on up to her low turtleneck and the mischief-making expression on her face. He didn't know what to make of this change in her, but she had torched his fuse.

"I see you went shopping." Quinn was doing her own checking, surprised by Teddy's slate-gray three-piece suit, white shirt and conservative gray-and-navy striped tie. He'd gotten his hair cut a little shorter, and he even had a dark gray topcoat over one arm. It was heartwarming to realize that he was trying to impress her family and their friends. He was doing, now, exactly what she'd wanted him to do when they'd first been married. It was puzzling, therefore, to realize that she wasn't certain that she was personally pleased with the change.

"I'm tapping my untapped potential." Teddy grinned, forever flip.

"I can see that." She was taking in the sharp knot in his tie. It was going to take her some time to get used to this new version of him.

Teddy kept to himself that he'd gone further than she could see. He'd spent hours in the library in the past week, ignoring work to brush up on current affairs, the political scene, memorizing whatever he thought he might be able to use for bright, intelligent chitchat. But all that was far from his mind at the moment.

"That is one treacherous dress!" He had his work cut out trying to keep his head on straight with her looking the way she was looking. Of all the nights she could have picked to be uncharacteristically bad, she would have to pick this one.

"That is a compliment, right?" Quinn bantered, knowing it was.

He wolf-whistled for her, rocking his own senses, as well. "Does that make it clear?"

"Uh-huh." Quinn flushed, but met his gaze straight-on. She'd been planning this shock to his system, and she was savoring it, knowing there was even more to come.

Groaning deep inside himself, Teddy tried to box his sexual frustration, which was carton-sized by now. "Do you want to tell me what you're up to?"

"I'm not up to anything." It was a lie. She was going to knock his socks off before she was through with him tonight.

Teddy brought forth a lazy smile. "My mother didn't raise any fools...."

"I'm not up to anything," Quinn repeated, pivoting to open the hall closet. She pulled out a black wool cape and took a long, pacing breath. Her heart was racing with excitement.

The long swatch of material, hooked at the nape of her neck, opened as she stretched. Teddy got a glimpse of her bare back. As best he could tell, she wasn't wearing a bra. Teddy bit down hard on his bottom lip, trying to hold on to his equilibrium. It was all he could do not to attack her.

Quinn clasped her cape, and picked up a small black clutch bag. "Let's go. I don't want us to be late." She had to get through the first part of the night before she could get to the second half.

Teddy reached out and opened the front door. He wasn't up to thinking like a gentleman, but he could behave outwardly like one—given that he had no other choice at the moment.

They weren't late, nor were they the first to arrive. A number of people were already mingling in the opulent living room, sipping cocktails and nibbling on canapés served by white-jacketed waiters. The decor was a blend of blues and greens, with touches of white and burnt orange. A white grand piano occupied one corner, leaving plenty of space. Multiple couches and club chairs were scattered about, interspersed with an array of marble and wood tables. Potted ferns created natural screens.

The senator spotted them and traversed the spacious expanse of thick green carpeting to make his way over to them. He gave his daughter an affectionate yet refined embrace.

Standing by, Teddy took a rough head count. There seemed to be eighteen or twenty people in the room. He hoped he wasn't biting off more than he could chew.

"You look different, Princess." The senator took a step back, holding both of Quinn's hands while he surveyed her.

Settling, Teddy felt an unexpected surge of one-sided camaraderie with him, seeing as how they were both confounded by Quinn's choice of attire. Women... Was there a man alive who could figure them out?

Quinn glanced around. "Where's Mom?"

"She'll be right out. She's in the kitchen checking something or another." The senator let go of his daughter's hands.

Teddy watched the Senator's right hand as it came his way. "Thank you for inviting me, sir." He gave the hand a firm shake.

"Teddy..." The Senator managed a smile.

Teddy tried to ascertain how he was measuring up in the senator's eyes. He spotted a flicker of curiosity while the senator appraised him. Teddy figured he couldn't be coming off too shabby if it was true that clothes made the man. The senator's suit was just about a duplicate of his own. However, his was off the rack, and the senator's was, no doubt, custom-made.

The senator answered a wave across the room with a lift of his hand. "Quinn, I know you know everyone here, but I'd like to introduce Teddy around."

Teddy wondered why he suddenly rated so much of the senator's goodwill. Of course, etiquette was etiquette....

Quinn swung her ginger-blond head toward Teddy. "We won't stay here very long," she whispered unceremoniously as they trotted behind her father. The senator was already several moves ahead of them.

Teddy returned a glance that said, "Thank you, in capital letters. He was trying to recall some of the snappy tidbits he'd recorded during the week, but all his mental processes had come to an abrupt halt. And the shoes he had bought this morning were killing his feet.

It took nearly three-quarters of an hour for William Barnett to make the rounds with his two charges. To Teddy, Quinn seemed more vivacious than he'd ever known her to be. He, on the other hand, could feel every cell in his body working feverishly to keep his sweat from showing.

A waiter passed nearby with a tray of drinks. Teddy grabbed one and gulped down a too-sweet cocktail with an orange-flavored base.

"Quinn, dear..." The greeting came from another one of her father's contemporaries—a distinguished-looking man with broad shoulders and a long, narrow face. His hair was almost white, but it was still full and curly. He wore glasses with maroon frames, each lens fifty percent bifocal.

Once more Quinn leaned forward for a light cheek-to-cheek exchange, ready to trade benign pleasantries.

The senator performed his duties. "Richard, this is Teddy Falco... Teddy, I'd like you to meet Judge Richard Klinger."

"It's very nice to meet you, Judge Klinger." Teddy was trying to keep track of names. He had the titles down pat. The men were all judges, attorneys or legislators. Their significant others came in a variety of sizes and shapes—all well-groomed and heavily perfumed.

Teddy turned a speculative eye on a chic brunette in ice-blue silk trousers as she stepped over to place a proprietary hand on the judge's shoulder. She didn't look to be more than thirty—thin and tanned, attractive rather than pretty. Either she was the judge's daughter or the judge liked them young.

"Chelsea, dear—" Klinger nodded judiciously, glowing beneath his matching winter tan "—I'd like you to meet Quinn Barnett and Teddy Falco."

"Mrs. Klinger," Quinn said, ending Teddy's guesswork. "I've been looking forward to meeting you." She'd been forewarned that the judge had remarried a woman barely half his age.

"Chelsea, please..." The new Mrs. Klinger put out a graceful hand. She'd adopted a model's stance, her other hand in the slant pocket of her ice-blue wool blazer.

Quinn offered a friendly smile. "Chelsea."

Teddy took his turn. "Hi."

Chelsea looked to her hubby. "Can I fix you a plate from inside?"

"Why don't we all go and have something to eat?" Senator Barnett suggested.

"Teddy?" Quinn asked.

"Sounds good to me," Teddy concurred. If he had his way, they'd spend the entire evening eating, instead of talking.

The adjoining dining room was almost as large as the living room. It was also a symphony of blues and greens, with lots of fresh flowers, which was nice.

The senator and the Klingers were drawn away by some other guests. Quinn and Teddy joined a line that was moving at a leisurely pace around the table. There was a buffet brimming with food.

"Quinn and Teddy!" Mrs. Barnett called musically.

Quinn and Teddy stepped out of line. Mother and daughter greeted each other with a sustained hug.

Teddy winged his best smile. "Thank you for including me." He squeezed the hand Mrs. Barnett presented. She was wearing a long dark green velvet sheath. Her hair was pulled back in a severe French knot. Teddy wondered if she was intentionally trying to blend in with the background.

"It's our pleasure to have you here," came the elegant Barnett reply.

Sincerity was all a matter of style, Teddy decided, gauging the interplay.

Edith Barnett gave the table a flurried glance. "Quinn, please go into the kitchen for me and tell them we're going to need more shrimp. I'm not getting along very well with the caterer. I always have trouble dealing with someone new."

To Teddy's surprise, he picked up the fact that beneath Edith Barnett's cultured veneer she was a bundle of nerves. Unexpectedly he found himself warming to her. He even thought of suggesting that he straighten the caterer out....

Quinn looked caringly after her mother as she fluttered away. "Get yourself something to eat. I'll be right back."

Teddy fixed himself a plate, sticking with foods that he could clearly identify. He avoided the shrimp, not wanting to make more of a dent in the tray.

Loitering in the dining room, Teddy waited for Quinn. He tried to make a production of his meal, hoping to look too engrossed to be singled out for small talk.

"I understand you're a promoter."

Teddy responded to Judge Klinger with a shake of his head. His mouth was full.

"What do you promote?" questioned a jowly-faced assemblyman, entering the conversation.

Teddy swallowed, forgoing a last chew. "Musicians, singers...mostly rock and roll."

"Ever think of entering the political arena?" The assemblyman forked a sliver of avocado on his plate. "Washington promoters make big bucks."

Quinn saw Teddy circled in conversation as she came back to the dining room. She filled a plate for herself and was just about to join him—or rescue him—when she was waylaid by friends of her parents who had just arrived.

It wasn't until much later in the evening that Quinn was able to link up with Teddy. She'd been shuffled from one group to another.

"I saw you talking to my father earlier." Quinn winced as she ushered Teddy to an unoccupied corner of the living room. She could just imagine what that had been like for the two of them.

"I have a confession to make." Teddy sported a grin. "I thought your parents were snobs, especially your father. But they're not snobs. They only want the best for their daughter, just like I'm going to want the best for our child." He was keyed up, but in a good way. He didn't have snobbery to fight—which would have been a losing battle. All he had to do was prove that he was the best for their little girl. He was fairly certain that he had made some progress tonight.

"I'm glad that you don't think they're snobs. Do you want to leave now? It's almost eleven." She was raring to go. "We've been here long enough."

"I'm fine—really. I'm having an okay time." Teddy swapped eye signals with Andrew Stevens, an attorney in the city, who was beckoning him over. They'd talked earlier about ecology and saving the earth. It was a topic that Teddy hadn't needed to brush up on. He had strong feelings on the subject.

"I'm glad that you're having an okay time, but I'd really like to leave now."

Suddenly worried, Teddy turned his eyes on Quinn. "Are you feeling all right?"

"I'm fine." Quinn smiled. "I just thought that we could do something more tonight."

"Like what?" He was watching her closely.

"Well...maybe, ah..." She wasn't very good at being coy. "We could go dancing."

It took Teddy a second to react. "You want to go dancing?"

"Yes." Quinn struggled to appear nonchalant.

"Well...sure..." Teddy slowly considered the curve she was throwing him. In all the time they'd been together, she'd never once suggested they go dancing. Museums, concerts, skiing, skating... All of that was more her speed.

"How about the Rainbow Room?" He could see himself slow-dancing with her, getting romantic. He liked that picture a whole lot.

"How about Levels?" Quinn wiggled her eyebrows at him.

Teddy's brown eyes widened. This wasn't a curve she was throwing at him. It was a keg of dynamite!

"How do you know Levels?"

"I just know," Quinn answered enigmatically. It was the club her dance instructor took her to for lessons, and she was all lessoned out....

"They hardly play any slow music there. It's mostly new wave." He hung out there sometimes, taking stock of new talent. He was certain that she didn't know what she thought she knew.

But apparently he was wrong.

"It's not just new wave. It's also rock and roll." She tugged his arm, catching sight of her parents. "Great... They're together."

They said a few more good-nights before they took their leave. When they were finally in the elevator, a very baffled Teddy said, "I would like to know how you know about Levels."

"I'm not going to tell you. I'm taking the Fifth," responded a closemouthed Quinn.

"You can't take the Fifth." Teddy's eyes flashed over Quinn, but she looked straight ahead.

"I can take the Fifth if I want to take the Fifth."

The elevator doors opened, and Quinn stepped briskly into the lobby.

Teddy was right at her side. "Fine...take the Fifth. Knock yourself out!" He didn't feel good about snapping at her. He was only doing it because she had him all confused.

"I'll tell you later." This wasn't working out the way she'd hoped. "When I tell you, I promise that you won't be mad, so could you stop being mad now?"

It was too cold to talk on the street on the way to the car. Teddy buffered Quinn. The wind whipped them both and tore at their hair.

"How about a hint?" Teddy pressed on doggedly, opening the Corvette's passenger door.

Quinn shook her head.

Teddy rounded the car, and got in himself. He started the ignition, eyed her for a second, then started to drive.

Quinn didn't endeavor to converse. Teddy was occupied with the running monologue going on in his head—not that he had anything particularly brilliant to tell himself. He did decide that she had better be factoring in jealousy with her promise.

As soon as they walked into Levels, Teddy realized he hadn't thought about the way he was dressed. He knew he had to look like a nerd. Quinn, on the other hand, fit right in.

Teddy took the cape Quinn swung at him and checked it with his topcoat. He guided her down the three steps to the first of the pits that gave Levels its name.

A light dawned in Teddy's head. "You didn't get dressed tonight for your father's dinner party. You got dressed for here," he accused lightly.

"That's right." Quinn took off just ahead of him, moving to the blast of high-energy rock with a loose-hipped swagger that Teddy was never going to forget.

Quinn halted at the border of the crowd at the enormous pecan-wood bar. Teddy, adrenaline pumping, found a single stool for her and parked his hip.

"Ginger ale?" Teddy asked in Quinn's ear. He was real tuned into her gig—whatever her gig was....

"Mmm," Quinn murmured. Her body rocked and rolled even after she was seated.

Teddy signaled to the bartender, Joey Lucas, a would-be actor who looked like a young Marlon Brando.

"Hey, Teddy." Joey came over to acknowledge the call. "Haven't seen you in a while."

"How've you been?" Teddy asked.

"Still pounding the beat." Joey smiled and gave Quinn a once-over. "The group we've got here now is not your speed. The keyboard player is in step, but the rest are just riding his coattails."

"I'm not here on business." Teddy cocked his head toward Quinn.

Quinn thanked her lucky stars that Teddy hadn't been here for a while. Had she known that he spent time here, she would have had her instructor take her elsewhere.

"Two ginger ales," Teddy ordered.

Joey poured them out.

Quinn took a shaky sip of her ginger ale. "That couple over there are good, aren't they?" She was motioning with her eyes.

Teddy took a quick look. "Not bad." He was more interested in watching her. They were speaking almost mouth-to-mouth in order to hear each other over the pulse of the music and the chatter of voices in their vicinity.

The ice cubes clinked against the side of Quinn's glass as she took another small swallow. "Have you ever promoted anyone from here?"

Teddy was becoming manic, waiting for whatever it was that was coming.... "No, but this is one of the places I stop in now and then for a look."

Quinn wanted to draw her heady feeling of anticipation out for as long as she could. "So, what do you think about the men's movement?"

"I didn't know there was one." Teddy followed Quinn's hands as she rubbed her arms. He guessed from the blush on her face that her action was more from restlessness than from chill. They were evenly matched on that score.

"Someone was telling me about it just tonight." Quinn tapped her nails on the polished surface of the bar.

"Well, I guess turnabout is fair play." Teddy smiled. "Does that mean that I get to wait for you to open doors?"

"I don't think so," Quinn rejoined.

The five-piece combo wound up their rock set and started to play something slow.

Teddy took advantage of the opening. "Shall we dance?"

Quinn listened for a moment. "To this?" She made a disdainful face.

Teddy laughed. "You don't like this song?"

"Not really."

"Okay..." Teddy chucked Quinn under her chin. It was the least physical touch he had in mind for her. "What would you like to dance to? I'll go slip the group a twenty."

"Let's just wait. I'm sure they'll play something soon." Quinn noticed her dance instructor just then. He was noticing her, too, as he came off the dance floor with a flashy blonde wrapped around him. Quickly Quinn shook her head, as briefly as she could and still get across a message not to approach her. She exhaled and blinked with relief as he changed direction.

Teddy was scrutinizing the track of Quinn's gaze. It seemed to him that she had a beam on a wiry, handsome dude who had been heading their way, strapped to a compact blonde.

"Have you got something in your eye, or are you flirting with someone?" The low, confidential tone of Teddy's voice had the steamy intensity of boiling water.

Quinn opted for the first choice. "I have something in my eye."

He glowered at her. "Let me have a look."

Quinn blinked her eyes again, rapidly. "It's out. Let's dance."

Teddy put a firm hand on Quinn's waist as she slipped from her stool. "They're still playing the same song."

"Yes." Quinn smiled sweetly. "It's grown on me."

Teddy got Quinn into a tight hold right at the fringe of the dance floor. She raised all-too-guileless eyes to him. If she knew he was angry, she was not letting on.

He led her in a small circle without speaking. They danced through three more slow tunes that completed the set. Then the music got hot, brash and heavy again. Teddy let Quinn go and started to leave the dance floor. He stopped after a few steps, realizing that she wasn't following him. He retraced his steps back to her.

"What now?"

"Let's keep dancing." Quinn gyrated, wiping every thought from Teddy's head. "Come on," she coaxed.

Teddy plowed a hand through his hair. He was dumbfounded, flabbergasted. His libido was bouncing through the roof.

"Don't I have it right?" Quinn asked bewitchingly, wiggling down and wiggling up.

"Oh, you have it right...." Teddy began to balance her act with some dishonorable hip motion of his own. "Where did this come from?"

Quinn ignored his question, baiting him. "Is this the best you can do?"

Teddy blew out a breath. "You want the full treatment?"

"You show me your stuff. I'll show you mine," Quinn said audaciously, giving him a taste of his own medicine.

"Come back to the bar with me for a minute."

With his grip on her elbow, Teddy steered Quinn off the dance floor.

"Does your doctor know that you're doing this?" Teddy demanded while he jerked off his tie and his jacket, dropping them both on a bar stool.

Quinn gave him a flippant smile. "He said the exercise is good for me."

Teddy rolled his sleeves and unbuttoned his vest. "In that case, get your motor running."

Quinn did, without trimming any curves.

And so did Teddy.

Teddy pulled Quinn flush up against his body as the combo broke. "Have you been holding out on me all along?"

Quinn shook her head, catching her breath against his shoulder. "Just the last few weeks. I've taken lessons...here... That guy you caught me looking at..."

With a grin, Teddy cut her off. "Was he your dance instructor?"

"Yes." Quinn smiled as they walked back to the bar.

"Why didn't you ask me?" Teddy picked up his jacket and tie. "I would have taught you." He couldn't stop the twinge of displeasure he felt thinking about her spending so much time with her good-looking dance instructor.

"I wanted to awe you."

Teddy shook his hand in a very Italian gesture. "Consider me awed."

"Consider me exhausted." She'd danced as much with her instructor, but the tension of showing off had worn her out.

"Sit here. I'll get the car."

"Teddy..." Quinn grabbed his arm. "Would you like to go with me the next time I go to the doctor?"

"Oh, Quinn..." He didn't give a hoot for propriety as he cradled the back of her head and gave her a kiss from his heart. She'd awed him again—even more this time.

Chapter Nine

Teddy raised the mug of coffee Angie had poured for him.

"How about a piece of cake?" Angie asked.

"No, thanks." Teddy produced a thin smile. "I'll just drink this and get out of your hair. I didn't know that Mom took the kids today to give you some time for yourself."

"Mom didn't take them to give me a day off. She took them to spoil them rotten. She doesn't think that Rick and I do a good enough job of that ourselves."

Teddy smiled again, but only briefly. "How's Rick?"

"Fine." Angie was giving Teddy a close examination. "How are things going with you and Quinn?"

Teddy looked at the kitchen table. "Great...just great."

"You must be tickled pink."

"That and every other color of the rainbow."

Angie arched a pert eyebrow. "Does that include black and blue?"

Teddy put his mug down and massaged his temples for a moment. "The truth is that it was going well, but now it's not going well. I just don't get it.... The harder I try, the more turned off she seems."

"Have you tried talking out your feelings with her?" Angie secured a crumb from the uncut cinnamon-filbert cake that she'd put on the table. She sucked it off her finger.

"You don't talk feelings to Quinn unless you're prepared to analyze them. Maybe I never read the right books. I can't analyze the way she can. All I know is that I'm crazy about her."

"Oh, Teddy. I don't want to see you getting your heart handed to you again."

Teddy smiled. "I'm a big boy. Don't worry."

"Quinn is due soon, isn't she?"

Teddy hacked out a breezy facade. "T minus nineteen days and counting."

Angie topped up Teddy's mug from the thermal pitcher of coffee on the table. "You said it was going well, and then it went wrong. What caused the change?"

Teddy shrugged his strong shoulders. "I can't figure it out. I've tried to be everything she wants me to be. When I'm around her, I'm a living, breathing miracle of Brooks Brothers fashion sense. I watch everything I say. I think before I speak. I've even trained myself to listen to some of the music she loves without nodding off. Some of it isn't half-bad."

"It sounds to me like you're trying to fake her out. Do you think that's the way to go?" He wasn't looking Brooks Brothers right now. He was wearing Nike sneakers that had seen better days. No socks. A well-fitting pair of old jeans, and a light yellow polo that advertised Coors beer.

Teddy took the offensive. "I don't consider it faking her out. I'm reinventing myself."

"Obviously that's not working," Angie countered.

"One side of my brain knows that. The other side says keep plugging away." Teddy sat tighter in his seat, tipping it backward and half off the floor.

"You know, Teddy, when women get this far along in their pregnancy they tend to be cranky. What Quinn is feeling may not have anything to do with you. I remember that I made Rick miserable both times. It's depressing when you can't see the shoes on your feet anymore. Men don't have any idea what it's like to look in a mirror and have a beached whale look back wearing your face."

Teddy smiled. "You never got that big, and Quinn isn't big, either. What you women fail to realize is that to the man who loves you, you're always gorgeous, especially when you're carrying his child."

Angie's mouth lifted in a grin. "That is the dumbest male rhetoric I've ever heard...."

Teddy nearly lost his balance. "You are a pistol. Do you know that?"

Angie returned a laugh. "Have you told Quinn recently that she's gorgeous?"

"Yes," Teddy responded on cue. "Only she doesn't seem to want compliments. Every time I say something nice to her she looks like she wants to haul off and slug me."

"That's because she doesn't believe you. And—" Angie paused "—you're the one who is responsible for making her look the way she looks. What do you want her to do? Thank you for it?"

Teddy was becoming exasperated. "What can I do? I'd carry the baby for her if I could."

"In a pig's eye!" Angie retorted. "If you say that to her, I hope she does slug you. Believe me, I would."

"I don't know why I came here. Rick deserves a medal for putting up with you."

Angie's reply to that comment was a Cheshire cat-style smile. Then she got back to the business at hand. "What Quinn probably needs is to be romanced. When was the last time you romanced her?"

Teddy had to meditate before he found an answer. "I was out of town for a while. When I got back we were busy wallpapering for the baby. We did her dressing room together, and my other bedroom..."

"That should have made the two of you feel close."

Teddy drummed his fingers on the table. "I'm pretty sure Quinn has changed her mind about the wallpaper, but she doesn't want to say so. It's another story, and I don't want to go into it. We've only got a thin truce going over that."

"All right. What about now? What have the two of you been doing lately?"

"Lamaze." Teddy set his chair back down. "Of course, we would get a Lamaze instructor who's a real winner... Talk about a woman knowing how to cut a guy off at his knees... Our first night, she declared that if men had to have babies it would be the end of the human race."

Angie held back a laugh. "Lamaze isn't every night."

"When it's not Lamaze, it's dinners with her parents, and dinners with Mom and Dad. We've hardly had any time alone."

"Make some time," Angie advised him. "And make it romantic."

"I was hoping lunch out would cheer you up," Allison said with a sigh.

"I'm sorry," Quinn apologized. "You're a pal for putting up with me."

Allison sliced and forked the twin lobster tails she'd ordered. "I'm a good listener. Why don't you try to tell me what's wrong?"

Quinn slouched in her seat ignoring her posture. It wasn't like her at all. "I don't know what's wrong. Sometimes I feel like I don't know who I am. It's like I'm not connected—not plugged in. I don't even know where the outlet is."

"Do you think that all this has to do with being pregnant?" Allison continued eating.

"I've had a very easy pregnancy. I'm scared about giving birth, but that's not it." Quinn took a taste of salmon, a taste of broccoli, and a little rice. She was concerned about eating from all the major food groups at every meal.

"You can tell me to butt out," Allison told her, "but I think you're moping around because you haven't sorted out your feelings about Teddy."

Quinn looked down at her plate. "How can I sort out my feelings about him? I don't even know who he is anymore. Right now, he's exactly the man I should have married."

Allison smiled. "You did marry him, Quinn, and you divorced him. I don't understand what you're trying to say."

Quinn's shoulders sagged. "I married the other Teddy Falco, not the new one. At first I thought this one was perfect for me. He looks like he'd be perfect for me. He acts like he'd be perfect for me, but we're not getting along. And the old one was completely wrong. Does this make any sense?"

"No." Allison shook her head. "Are you saying that Teddy is trying to be more of what you want him to be, but now that he is, you don't like it?"

"I don't dislike it, but I don't like it the way I should like it." Quinn sighed unhappily.

Allison put her fork down for a second. "Maybe you haven't had enough relationships to figure out what you're looking for."

Quinn thought about it. She hadn't been inexperienced when she'd met Teddy Falco. There had been a couple of significant men in her life. Neither had made her see stars in the daytime the way he could.

"That's not it," Quinn answered with conviction.

Allison dabbed butter from her lips with her napkin. "He's wild about you."

Quinn leaned forward, giving the impression that she was imparting a secret. "I'm wild about him, too."

"Which one are you wild about?"

Quinn rolled her lips together. "Both of them, I guess."

"Are you two—?" Allison waved her fork.

Quinn knew what Allison was getting at. "My doctor said no sex from now on. Anyway, we haven't since the divorce. We did come very close a number of times, before I became a hippo. I haven't tempted him for quite some time."

"Does he still tempt you?"

Quinn's cheeks reddened. "Let's eat."

"Where are we going?" Quinn asked, sitting as easily as she could in Teddy's "muscle" car.

"I'm surprising you." Teddy smiled lazily. "You'll see when we get there."

Quinn didn't know why, but she had butterflies in her stomach. They'd been multiplying since he'd called her and told her he was taking her out for a special night. An hour after his call, she'd received a hand delivered package from Lord and Taylor with a soft, billowy dress that he'd purchased for her to wear. Wonder of wonders, it was simple enough, with its shirred yoke and capped sleeves, to suit her tastes, and fancy enough to work well with his white jacket and tuxedo pants. She guessed that he'd taken her literally when she'd said she hated buying clothes at this point in her pregnancy.

Teddy's eyes were back on Quinn. "Did I tell you how beautiful you look?"

"Yes." Quinn smiled. Her hands crunched the hand-crocheted white cardigan in her lap. "Thank you again for the dress. I love it." She felt as beautiful as a woman could feel toting around a watermelon in her belly.

Teddy propped his elbow at the opened window and put his hand on the roof. It was a balmy first-of-July night. "I love you in pink."

Quinn meet Teddy's gaze, and they stared at each other for a hushed second of breathless appreciation, neither missing anything.

Teddy brought his hand in from the roof of the car to hold the wheel while he patted his black bow tie, checking to be sure it was still holding straight. He felt like a teen again—out on his first prom.

He's as nervous as I am! Quinn realized, pleased that they were both at the same level for a change. Had the issue been that they couldn't seem to align with each other? Was that what had caused her to become out of sorts with him?

Quinn promised herself that she wasn't going to be out of sorts with him tonight...no matter what....

Teddy angled another glance at Quinn. "I can turn the air-conditioning on and close the windows, if you like."

Quinn shook her head. The breeze from her open window played with her hair, swishing her bangs off her forehead. She was watching street numbers, trying to figure out where he was taking her. They were heading uptown along Broadway.

Teddy turned east in the seventies.

Quinn couldn't think of a restaurant or club along here. "Are we supposed to be at the boat basin?" she asked, looking around, confused.

"Yes" was all Teddy offered. He was busy watching for the right slip. Finding it, he gave the wheel a sharp turn, slowed and parked.

Quinn studied their surroundings again before she met the smile on Teddy's face. "This is a private boat basin."

"Yes." He gave her one of his outlaw grins. "What do you think of that yacht over there?"

"It's very nice." Quinn eyed the streamlined white cruiser anchored in the foamy lap of the Hudson River.

"It's ours for tonight." Teddy opened his door, lunged out and came around to her side.

Quinn had to help Teddy assist her out of the car. It took both of them to accomplish the feat. "Who owns it?" Quinn asked, once she was standing. Her eyes were bright.

"Someone I know. He let me borrow it, complete with a crew. I'm taking you for a cruise."

"Where are we going?"

"You name it. I'll take you anywhere you like." Teddy wrapped Quinn in a hug, locking his fingers low at the small of her back. She filled his arms.

Quinn laughed. "Teddy, be serious!"

Teddy stole a quick nip at her neck. "We're going to sail around Manhattan, but there's no reason we can't pretend. Come on, live dangerously with me."

"I don't have to pretend to live dangerously when I'm with you. You are a hazard," Quinn said, still smiling.

Teddy gave Angie a silent thank-you for shoving him in the right direction. "Ready to go on board?"

"Yes," Quinn breathed, excited.

Teddy held Quinn firmly as they walked up the gangway. She was wearing thick, low-heeled white pumps and didn't need as much support as he was giving her. But she did like it ...

The very first thing Quinn noticed, once they were on deck, was the all-male trio—keyboard player, saxophonist and guitarist.

Teddy gave a nod, and the group began a medley of Billy Joel hits. The three sang "She's Always A Woman." They were playing on the cuff tonight. He'd promised to give them a serious audition during the week.

Teddy strung his arm around Quinn's shoulders, hoping the music he'd selected was going to strike the right chord. "They take requests."

Quinn turned her shining face to Teddy. "Let's dance."

Teddy held back for a second. "Put your sweater on."

Quinn dropped her white clutch bag on a lounge chair. She put her sweater on without protest, though she didn't need the extra warmth.

Teddy swept Quinn into an embrace. He got as close to her as he could with their child between them, keeping their hips apart.

Neither was aware when the gangway was raised and the yacht started to cruise. Teddy hummed in Quinn's ear. Quinn purred the words to "Just the Way You Are" against Teddy's cheek. It didn't matter to either of them that they were both off-key.

"I want you so badly, Quinn," Teddy half groaned against her hair. It amazed him that he could still have fantasies about a woman who was almost due to deliver a child. He hadn't thought, until now, that it was okay for him to tell her.

"I want you, Teddy." Quinn moved her mouth along his jaw.

"You brat," Teddy teased, skirmishing to keep himself in neutral. "We both know that I have to stay harmless."

"But I still mean it." Quinn raised mischievous eyes, and they both laughed.

Teddy lightly swatted Quinn's bottom.

"Teddy!" Quinn stepped back. "The musicians are watching us."

"No, they're not," Teddy quipped, reeling her back where she belonged. "I told them ahead of time that they can't look."

"In that case..." Quinn brought her arms to his neck, then closed her eyes as Teddy's mouth descended. He seemed more like his old self tonight. She still didn't know how to match herself to him other than physically, but this Teddy was the one she recognized. He was the one that brought out her ardor.

Maneuvering with the brakes on, Teddy kept the kiss gentle. Still, the pleasure of it assailed them, and they stayed with it long enough that it robbed them both of their breath.

Teddy swiveled Quinn in a slow, sexy circle while she kept her arms entwined around his neck. "So, where are we heading?" he asked.

"Heading?" Her throat was all clotted with feelings.

"Where would you like to pretend that this yacht is taking us?"

Quinn didn't have to think. "St. Thomas."

"Quinn..." Teddy whispered, and his eyes slid shut.

Quinn closed her eyes, as well. "I wasn't as uptight on your motorcycle as I let you think," she disclosed. "I wanted to hang on to you."

"You little imp!" Teddy laughed. "You had me out of control."

"I know." Quinn batted her eyes, remembering her breasts pressed against his strong back, the warm wind on her cheeks, the hardness of his muscles bunched up at each turn.

"I should fix you good for that," Teddy countered raggedly.

"I wish you could," Quinn vamped, behaving with him in a way she would never have considered behaving with anyone else.

"Excuse me, sir..." Quinn and Teddy were interrupted by one of the crew, a gray-haired man in a cropped white jacket and dark pants. "Sir, the chef has dinner ready to be served."

It wasn't easy for Teddy to separate himself from Quinn. "I hope you're hungry."

"We both are." Quinn touched her belly.

Teddy clasped Quinn's hand as they were led aft, with tantalizing aromas wafting their way. The sun, setting on the sea, brushed the horizon with a glow. Quinn's eyes sought Teddy's. She didn't have to say anything for him to know where her mind was. They were both recalling the moonlight over St. Thomas. It was all Teddy could do to remind himself that he had to stay civilized. He would much rather ravish her than a meal.

The food was delicious. Teddy had left the menu to the chef, requesting only that there be imported bottled water in an ice-filled bucket to simulate champagne. She no longer seemed to want ginger ale.

They began with shrimp cocktails in an glazed orange sauce. There was chicken teriyaki, and ginger-laced rice. Jumbo scallops sautéed in lemon butter. Broiled swordfish with broccoli hollandaise. Homemade fettuccine with crabmeat.

Quinn and Teddy's mouths stayed engaged in chewing, as they were both attempting to subjugate their need for each other.

"There's garlic in the fettuccine," Teddy pointed out for Quinn. "You may want to pass on it." He remembered her once saying that she didn't care for garlic.

Quinn smiled and licked hollandaise from her lips. "It may have something to do with my pregnancy, but I seem to have acquired a taste for garlic." She helped herself to a serving.

Teddy smiled. "That's my son making his presence known."

"Or your daughter." Quinn twirled a forkful of fettuccine against a tablespoon, as she'd seen Teddy do.

Teddy watched, enjoying her Italianized motion. "I'm having a son. Didn't I tell you?"

Quinn's eyes widened. "Did Dr. Wextler tell you something he didn't tell me? I thought we agreed not to ask after the amniocentesis. Did he tell you we're having a boy?"

"I didn't ask." Teddy grinned. "He didn't tell me."

"What is this? Something like the Italian thunderbolt?"

"Something like that."

Quinn went back to twirling her fettuccine. "Personally, I think it's a girl."

"One of us is bound to be right." Teddy took the fork from Quinn and fed her the fettuccine.

"I can't eat another bite," Quinn said after she'd swallowed and chewed three mouthfuls.

Their waiter, the same crew member who had directed them to the table, stepped forward. He'd stayed to the side, but within earshot. "Shall I have the table cleared?"

"Yes," Teddy responded.

"The chef has cappuccino and zabaglione for dessert. Would you like that now, or later?"

"Later," Teddy answered, helping Quinn out of her chair.

They held hands as they walked to the rail. Sunset had turned to night. Quinn stared out toward the sea, and at the skyline of Manhattan, bathed in moonlight. Teddy kept his gaze on her profile. The luscious food, the wonderful music, the beautiful setting, all paled in comparison to the romance that was going on between Quinn and Teddy.

"The baby is kicking," Quinn murmured softly.

"Can I feel?"

"Yes."

Teddy placed his wide palm to the swell of Quinn's stomach, fondling her seekingly. Quinn let his hand trail unchecked while they both willed their child to move again. When it did, she saw the reverent exaltation on his face.

"Does it hurt?" He was ashamed to realize that he'd never asked her before now.

Quinn heard Teddy's breathing become suddenly anxious. "No," she answered, quick to reassure him.

The baby rolled within the solid wall of her belly against its father's hand.

"He, or she, seems to be getting to know you." Quinn smiled.

"I'm going to teach him to play ball, and swim... You can teach us both to ski."

Quinn looked into Teddy's eyes. Their faces were lit satiny by the deck's low-intensity floodlights. "Do you promise to let me teach you to ski?"

"Name the vow you want, and I'll give it to you."

"Your word will do."

"You have my word." He would have reached for the moon if that had been what she wanted.

Quinn drifted along, feeling connected, in contact with Teddy's tenderness. She wasn't at all in the mood to do much in the way of thinking.

The air became chilled, and Quinn shivered slightly. Teddy was quick to take his jacket off. "Put it on."

Quinn objected. "You'll be cold."

"I won't be." Her reaction to him tonight was all the body heat he needed.

Quinn stopped fighting.

The sleeves were much too long, but Teddy folded them up to her wrists. He took hold of the lapels, meaning to wrap them together, but she looked like such an urchin that he couldn't resist taking a kiss from her first.

With the tip of his tongue, Teddy tasted the salt the water's spray had brought to her lips. He ran his hands up and down her back, cradling the periphery of her blossomed stomach with his forearms as his palms came to a rest at the sides of her breasts.

Teddy ended the kiss long before Quinn wanted him to. He gazed at her face, telling her with his eyes how much difficulty he was having keeping himself disciplined.

"Maybe we should have the cappuccino now," Quinn suggested, drowsy and dreamy.

Teddy brought Quinn back to the table, and they had two cups each. Though they were sated, they still managed to taste the zabaglione.

"You're tired," Teddy said when he caught Quinn trying to hold back a yawn.

"A little," Quinn admitted.

Teddy saw to it that the yacht headed back to the basin.

"Thank you for a wonderful night," Quinn said later, as Teddy drove her home.

Teddy smiled at her. "Lie back and rest."

Quinn closed her eyes and just about fell asleep when Teddy stirred her with his hand. "Home," he whispered, having found a place to park almost at the door of her building.

Quinn rubbed her eyes with the backs of her hands and sat up, waiting for Teddy to come around for her. They kept their arms slung around each other all the way up in the elevator. Teddy took the key from Quinn and opened her front door. Quinn stepped into Teddy's arms as soon as he'd closed the door behind them.

Teddy halted the kiss that was coming. ''Will you marry me, Quinn?'' He smiled, already knowing her answer.

Quinn's lips quivered. ''No, Teddy.''

Chapter Ten

"What have you been doing all night?" Teddy questioned acerbically. "Playing?"

Propelled by the sudden ache low in her back and the despair welling up in her heart, Quinn walked into the living room and sat down on the couch. She hadn't wanted to hurt him.

Teddy followed after her but stayed on his feet. He regarded her in stone-cold silence.

Quinn returned a wilted look. "Teddy, please try to understand. I'm so mixed up. I wish someone would just tell me what to do."

"I'll tell you what to do. Marry me." His voice was tight and volatile. He knew he should take a hike, but he couldn't get himself to go.

"Don't do this, Teddy."

"Do what?"

"Push me."

"Push you," Teddy repeated angrily. "I've been dancing around you in circles for months with my fist jammed down my throat."

"I don't want it to end for us," Quinn pleaded. "Why can't we just stay the way we are?"

"That's an interesting prospect." Teddy fumed. "Exactly what are we?"

"Best friends, parents..." Quinn sat braced, experiencing muscle cramps in her belly, along with the continuing ache in her back.

"How about lovers? Are we going to be lovers, too?"

"We've tried marriage, Teddy. Neither one of us knows how to make it work."

"You never tried, Quinn."

"I did try. I wanted it to work."

Disgust etched Teddy's features. "If you'd really intended for us to have a marriage, you would have made a total commitment. But you didn't do that. You made up your mind right at the start that it wasn't going to work."

"I did make a commitment to you. I tried as hard as you did." Quinn gripped her arms in front of her distended belly and rocked forward. She was certain the discomfort she was feeling had everything to do with tension.

"That's a laugh! If you'd truly made a commitment to our marriage, you would have sold your apartment when you moved into my loft. You didn't sell it, because you figured you were going to need it again. I congratulate you for playing it smart. It can be hairy to find a decent condo with a good address."

Quinn had tears in her eyes. "I was not thinking that way."

"What do you want, Quinn? What do you want from a guy?"

"Please, Teddy. Let's not say things just to hurt each other...."

"Why not? We're evenly matched on that score...." Teddy shrugged sullenly. "You want to know what really blows my brain cells?"

Quinn compressed her lips. She had no doubt that he was going to tell her.

"I've been turning myself inside out for you. I've been improving myself. I've been trying to be everything you've ever wanted me to be. Boy, what a jerk that makes me!" Teddy prowled around the room, unable to stand still anymore.

"Did I ever ask you to change?" Quinn took a deep breath as her stomach cramping turned to pain. "I never asked you to change."

He whirled around to indict her face-to-face. "You asked me, Quinn. You asked me in a thousand different ways without having to put it into words. But hey, listen, that's okay. You gave me a no. I can take a no."

"Teddy..." Quinn braved a glance at him, but quickly veered her eyes away. "You make it impossible for me to sort through my feelings."

"Maybe you should try not to sort, and just feel. You might get to liking it."

"I was just feeling when I married you, and look where it got us." Quinn swiped at the corners of her eyes with her knuckles, then went back to clutching her arms. "You try to make things go the way you think they should, but when they don't, they don't. We've got to be honest with each other.''

"*You* want to *believe* you're being honest. *You* want to *believe* that we can't make it work. That's what makes it easier for you to keep running away. You're terrified of your emotions. You're terrified of trying to blend with me. You're terrified that somehow you're going to lose your independence. Try that honesty on for size...."

"You always think that you have all the answers," Quinn yelled. "But you don't have all the answers."

"I'm not saying that I've got all of them...but I've got a few. You know how you're going to wind up, Quinn? You're going to wind up meeting some guy as suppressed as you, and you're going to delude yourself into believing you're in love. But you won't feel satisfied—not deep down.... You'll go looking for someone to make you come alive for an hour at a time. That guy won't be me, Quinn.... I don't want to be your stud on the side...."

"You're a bastard, Teddy. You're a—" Quinn pounded a fist against her leg. "Just look what you're making me say.... I don't say words like that. I don't even think them. Never!"

Teddy flashed his insolence at her. "I guess you should never say never."

Quinn watched him start for the hall. She wanted to stop him. This conversation wasn't over as far as she was concerned. She had more to say before she finished telling him off.

"Let's just stay out of each other's way until the baby comes" was the last remark Teddy made before he crashed out the front door, shutting it behind him with a bang.

The tears Quinn had been fighting came full-force, bursting into a torrent. She wiped her face over and over again with one hand. Her other hand was still on her stomach.

Quinn needed to blow her nose. One-handed, she felt around for her handbag and worked open the clasp to pull out a tissue. A sudden acute stab in her belly made her gasp and hold her breath until it subsided.

Quinn gingerly blew her nose and then made her way to her bedroom, walking slowly. She did give a thought to the possibility that she was in labor, but it was still more than two weeks before her due date. She'd been told that it wasn't uncommon to have an episode of false labor. Dr. Wextler had told her that if that was to happen she should rest and give it a chance to play itself out.

"Yes?" Teddy said into the receiver. He was braced on an elbow, hazy at being awoken from his sleep.

Quinn's voice was all wobbly. "My water broke. The pains are about eight minutes apart. I called Dr. Wextler. He said to come in. I wasn't sure if I should call you...."

Teddy flung off his covers and sat bolt upright. "Don't move, Quinn. Don't do anything. I'll be right there."

Teddy pulled on jeans, stuffed his feet into sneakers and dropped a T-shirt over his head. He drove like a madman, leaving his car in the middle of the street once he got to her building.

He didn't have the patience to wait for the elevator. Instead, he took the stairs three at a time to her floor.

Her door was locked, and Teddy cursed because he didn't have a key. Quinn heard his knock from the living room. She shuffled her way to the door and undid the locks for him.

She was trembling uncontrollably. Teddy scooped her up off her feet and into his arms. It was hard to tell where her quavering ended and his shaking began.

"My suitcase," she screamed when he turned to walk out, carrying her.

"I'll bring it to you tomorrow." He was giving it his all to keep his voice steady.

"No." Quinn wiggled against his hold. "I want it now.... I'm not going without my suitcase! Put me down. I can walk."

Being excruciatingly careful, Teddy set Quinn on her feet. "Where is it?" he groaned.

Quinn leaned against the wall just outside her apartment. "It's right next to my bed."

Teddy charged like an animal after Quinn's suitcase. He came back with it in seconds. "Can we go now?"

"Yes, just lock my door. My bag is on the couch. The key is in there."

Teddy was at his wits' end, but he followed Quinn's instructions to keep her appeased. He locked the door, picked her suitcase up and reached for her.

"Wait," Quinn said between pains. "I want to take my handbag with me. My lipstick is in there, and my powder and blush—" She caught her breath as the pain came again. "Open the door...."

"You don't need makeup. You've never needed makeup. Please, babe. Please, let's get to the hospital." Teddy was babbling to himself as much as to her.

"Okay." Quinn nodded, unable to catch her breath.

Somehow Teddy got her to the elevator. It felt like hours to him before the doors opened.

There was a patrol car parked in front of his Corvette. An officer had a flashlight on his back license plate, getting ready to write him up.

"We're having a baby," Teddy called out, deliriously happy to see a cop. "We've got to get to the hospital."

The officer reconnoitered quickly. "The two of you can get in the back seat of the patrol car. I can get you there faster. My partner can drive your car. Which hospital are you going to?"

"Lenox Hill...Seventy-seventh and Park," Teddy answered, with Quinn digging her nails into his arm. She was holding on to him for dear life.

The officer spoke to his partner, who immediately got out of the passenger seat. Teddy tossed the second officer his car keys. The first officer took Quinn's small suitcase and put it up front. Clumsily Teddy managed to get Quinn into the back seat and then came around to join her from the other side. He banged his head getting in, but was too distracted to feel the pain.

"This is horrible," Quinn moaned, clinging to Teddy. She thought she was going to die.

"I know, baby...." Teddy crooned. "It will be over soon. Breathe with me, Quinn. Please, breathe with me.... Inhale... Let it out slow. Pant, pant, pant..."

"I didn't want us to be fighting when the baby came," Quinn cried, panting.

Teddy hated himself for having picked this night, of all nights, to start in on her. He hated himself for everything he'd said. "I'm sorry," he told her over and over again, panting with her. "I didn't mean it."

Quinn grabbed Teddy's hand hard, forgetting about her breathing. "Will you be unhappy if it's a girl?"

"No, Quinn, no," Teddy murmured. "I'm going to love having a daughter."

Her eyes as she turned them to him were dazed. She was in agony. "I keep praying that the baby will be healthy," she whispered, touching his heart anew.

"It will be. I promise." He was becoming crazed, seeing her this way. Whether she wanted it or not, he was going to make sure that she was given something for the pain once they got to the hospital. "Breathe with me, Quinn," he implored her.

She did it with him as the next contraction took over, and kept it up as the officer put his siren on, securing a clear path as they hit some traffic.

Finally, they made it to the hospital. A nurse brought a wheelchair out from the emergency room entrance after the officer dashed in to brief the on-duty staff.

"It's coming out!" Quinn screamed, looking frantically at Teddy, who was at her side. A nurse was wheeling from behind, bringing Quinn backward into an elevator.

"No, it isn't. Don't push. We'll have you in the delivery room in just a minute," the nurse said, exercising authority in a sedate tone.

Dr. Wextler was already there and waiting with three nurses in operating room garb. He helped Teddy get Quinn from the chair to the table.

"Hurry up..." Quinn kicked up a fuss while the nurses worked as fast as they could to take off her maternity slacks, her panties, and the blouse she'd put on braless.

"Take it easy." Dr. Wextler tried to get Quinn to relax as best she could and told her to pant as he went to wash his hands.

Quinn became even more unruly when one of the nurses tightened the belt of a monitor just as another contraction ripped through her.

Teddy stood to one side, holding Quinn's hand, though he didn't think she was aware of him. He stared, big-eyed and shaky-legged, looking down at her, sweating as her muscles tensed, changing the contours of her distended abdomen. He swore silently at himself for doing this to her.

"I want her to have something for the pain," he insisted adamantly.

Quinn shook her head furiously. Dr. Wextler and the nurses exchanged glances. "She's going to have the baby before anything we give her will take effect." It was the doctor who responded, while one nurse dropped a sheet over Quinn and another set her legs up in stirrups.

"I told you it was coming now," Quinn said, and she almost smiled at Teddy, feeling vindicated.

Teddy leaned over to smooth her hair back from her forehead. She gazed up at him, and actually did smile. "You look like you're turning green," she said, free of pain for a second. Then, her lips clenched. Her eyes closed, and she raised a hand over her head, the fingers curled into a fist.

"You can start to push with the next contraction," Dr. Wextler said, positioned on a stool between Quinn's raised legs.

"Keep her forehead cool with the washcloth," a nurse instructed Teddy, pointing out a bowl half filled with water and ice.

Another nurse, sitting before the monitor screen, added, "I'll let you know when each contraction begins. When I say the word, you tell her to push, and help her pant."

The third nurse contacted Teddy with her eyes. "You can rub her belly lightly. It helps sometimes."

The nurse at the monitor nodded to Teddy. "Here we go."

"Push, baby, push," Teddy begged, feather-stroking Quinn's stomach and mopping her head. He was pale and discombobulated, but somehow or other he was getting his part done.

"I'm pushing!" Quinn snapped at Teddy. "You're getting water in my eyes...."

"I'm sorry, baby... I'm sorry... Pant, pant, pant."

It took Quinn and Teddy ten minutes to get a rhythm going. She pushed and moaned. He groaned and felt sympathetic pains in his gut. He wiped her temple, making sure the cloth was wrung. He backhanded his own forehead. Together, they panted in unison.

Twenty minutes later, Dr. Wextler announced, "The head is out. Lots of hair. A few more pushes and we'll see what we've got here."

Teddy gentled the wide base of Quinn's stomach, and without hearing himself he affixed the word *almost* to his litany. And Quinn smiled up at him in between pains.

Four contractions later, Dr. Wextler trumpeted, "It's a boy...."

"Is he healthy?" Quinn asked weakly, while Teddy gripped the side of the delivery table to keep his balance.

"He's perfect," Dr. Wextler answered, and the child seconded him with a powerful wail.

"Can I see him?" There were tears of joy streaming down Quinn's face.

"In just a moment." Dr. Wextler was handing their son to a pediatric nurse, who had walked in at some point without Quinn and Teddy noticing. She cleaned, measured, weighed and checked out their bundle of joy.

"Eight pounds, ten ounces... twenty-two inches," the pediatric nurse called out to the new parents. Then she brought the baby to Quinn, who couldn't breathe as she held him against her stomach.

"He's so beautiful," Teddy said in a hoarse voice. Then he remembered she'd wanted a girl. "Is it okay that it's a boy?"

"I wanted a son so bad." Quinn smiled beautifully. "He looks like you.... I wanted him to look like you...."

A nurse took the baby from Quinn. "She's going to sleep now. Why don't you go make some phone calls, *Dad?* You'll be able to see her a little later in her room."

Teddy gazed once more at Quinn. "Thank you," he said to her, but she was already fading off into blissful sleep.

Teddy made all the calls he could think of. It was five-thirty in the morning, but no one complained about being roused from sleep. He looked in at his son from outside the nursery. A nurse lifted him and brought him up to the window. He was wrapped tight in a soft blue blanket. Teddy stood there making goofy faces at his son. And the baby opened his eyes and stared at him, as though annoyed that he was being disturbed. Teddy studied him in wonder. He was a miracle beyond anything Teddy had ever dreamed of. He yearned to touch him, but he was more than petrified at the thought.

Quinn opened heavy-lidded eyes and found Teddy dozing in a chair near her bed. His cheek was propped on one hand. His hair was disheveled, and he needed a shave. Feeling euphoric, and hazy, Quinn listened to the cadence of his breathing.

"Teddy," she said after a while. Her voice was thick and fuzzy.

Teddy's eyes flew open, and he sprang out of the armchair. "You're awake," he said softly, standing next to her and taking her hand.

"Not fully," Quinn mumbled. "I want to be wide awake." Her eyes drifted closed again.

Teddy waited with bated breath. When she didn't open her eyes, he sat down again, but he couldn't go back to sleep. He was content just to look at her.

"Teddy?"

"I'm here."

"I need to talk to you." This time, when Quinn opened her eyes, she was more focused.

"We can talk later, after you've rested some more."

"No, now." Quinn pushed herself up a little. Teddy was there instantly to fix the pillows behind her shoulders and head.

"I spoke with your mother and your father." Teddy smiled at her. "They're thrilled. 'I'm a Grandpa,' your father kept saying. 'How do you like that? I'm a Grandpa.'"

Quinn giggled. "What about your mother and father? What did they say?"

"Say?" Teddy grinned. "They did a jig. We've given them their first grandson. They'll all be here later."

"Teddy?"

"Yes, Quinn."

"I did a lot of thinking tonight, and do you know what I realized?"

"What, Quinn?"

"You make me breathe right. I don't breathe right when I'm not with you. I want to breathe right all the time. Will you help me to breathe right?"

Teddy wondered if they'd given her something in the delivery room after he'd left. She wasn't making sense, but he was happy to humor her.

"I'll always help you breathe right."

Quinn closed her eyes, then opened them. "I don't want a big wedding. I want a quick one. Okay? When will they bring the baby in?" Her eyes closed then, and she was out like a light.

Teddy wasn't sure how much time had passed when Quinn's eyes blinked wide once more and she lifted her head. It could have been anywhere from fifteen minutes to half an hour. His head was spinning.

"I did tell you, didn't I?" she questioned, sounding more alert.

"About, uh..." His voice trailed off.

Quinn was on the brink of asking him if something was the matter, when he blurted, "About getting married?"

Quinn smiled happily. "Only I don't want your new, improved version. I want your old one back."

"You want the one who drives you nuts?" He was afraid to move—afraid the slightest jar and his brain would go out of commission.

"That's the one." Quinn was regarding Teddy nervously now. He didn't seem to be having any reaction to her declaration of love. "You haven't lost him, have you?"

"Oh, no. He's still here." Teddy clamped his hands to his thighs. "Quinn, I understand what's happening. You just had a baby, and you're feeling emotional."

"Oh..." She had a clear picture now. "You think I'm going to change my mind."

"Are you?" It was exactly what he was thinking.

"No." Quinn shook her head. "Did you change your mind?"

Teddy shook his head. It was the only part of his body that moved. "What made you decide?"

"I did a lot of thinking tonight." Quinn's expression turned worldly. "I was the one who was changing. Then you were changing, and we weren't in sync. I'm not going to be just like you, but that's okay. We can be different, and I can compromise without feeling that you're taking over. Neither one of us has to give anything up. We're probably going to fight sometimes, but we can always make up.''

Teddy's heart was laboring hard in his chest. ''When did you get all this thinking done? You were pretty busy tonight.''

Quinn didn't know why Teddy was wasting so much time with explanations. She was anxious to get to the part where they kissed. ''I figured it out after you left...up until my water broke. Then I stopped thinking about it.'' Quinn had a new thought. ''Remember to call Bloomingdale's and tell them we're only going to need one of everything.... And would you call the manager's office at my condo? Tell him it's available. I know they have a waiting list.''

That was the remark that brought Teddy to his feet. ''You really mean this!''

Quinn laughed. ''Haven't you been listening?''

The answer he gave her was the one she'd been needing. He sat down on the side of her bed and drew her into his arms.

Quinn put a finger to Teddy's mouth, teasingly keeping them apart. ''I just want to be sure I'm getting the old Teddy Falco.''

Teddy grinned. ''Get your finger out of my way before I bite it off.''

Quinn cooperated ecstatically, giving herself up to his tempestuous kiss while she ran her fingers through the shaggy thickness of his hair. Their lips were fevered and demanding. They didn't care to check themselves.

"I've decided that I may as well still be your stud, even if it's legal," Teddy quipped, a breath away from Quinn's swollen lips.

"Six weeks." Quinn put a hand alongside Teddy's rough jaw. "I asked."

"I'm already berserk," Teddy grumbled before he kissed her again and dealt with the restriction.

"We're going to have to get used to it. I'd like to have at least three more."

Teddy groaned, and rolled his eyes. "You've got to be kidding!"

Quinn laughed. "There's no compromising on that. Now, could you go find a nurse, and tell her to bring in our son? We still haven't finished arguing about a name. I don't know what's wrong with TJ. Teddy Junior is a perfect name...."

* * * * *

Is your father a Fabulous Father?

Then enter him in Silhouette Romance's

"FATHER OF THE YEAR" Contest
and you can both win some great prizes! Look for contest details in the FABULOUS FATHER titles available in June, July and August...

ONE MAN'S VOW by Diana Whitney
Available in June

ACCIDENTAL DAD by Anne Peters
Available in July

INSTANT FATHER by Lucy Gordon
Available in August

Only from

SRFD

OFFICIAL RULES • MILLION DOLLAR BIG WIN SWEEPSTAKES
NO PURCHASE OR OBLIGATION NECESSARY TO ENTER

To enter, follow the directions published. **ALTERNATE MEANS OF ENTRY:** Hand-print your name and address on a 3"×5" card and mail to either: Silhouette Big Win, 3010 Walden Ave., P.O. Box 1867, Buffalo, NY 14269-1867, or Silhouette Big Win, P.O. Box 609, Fort Erie, Ontario L2A 5X3, and we will assign your Sweepstakes numbers (Limit: one entry per envelope). For eligibility, entries must be received no later than March 31, 1994 and be sent via 1st-class mail. No liability is assumed for printing errors or lost, late or misdirected entries.

To determine winners, the sweepstakes numbers on submitted entries will be compared against a list of randomly preselected prizewinning numbers. In the event all prizes are not claimed via the return of prizewinning numbers, random drawings will be held from among all other entries received to award unclaimed prizes.

Prizewinners will be determined no later than May 30, 1994. Selection of winning numbers and random drawings are under the supervision of D.L. Blair, Inc., an independent judging organization whose decisions are final. One prize to a family or organization. No substitution will be made for any prize, except as offered. Taxes and duties on all prizes are the sole responsibility of winners. Winners will be notified by mail. Chances of winning are determined by the number of entries distributed and received.

Sweepstakes open to persons 18 years of age or older, except employees and immediate family members of Torstar Corporation, D.L. Blair, Inc., their affiliates, subsidiaries and all other agencies, entities and persons connected with the use, marketing or conduct of this Sweepstakes. All applicable laws and regulations apply. Sweepstakes offer void wherever prohibited by law. Any litigation within the province of Quebec respecting the conduct and awarding of a prize in this Sweepstakes must be submitted to the Régies des Loteries et Courses du Quebec. In order to win a prize, residents of Canada will be required to correctly answer a time-limited arithmetical skill-testing question. Values of all prizes are in U.S. currency.

Winners of major prizes will be obligated to sign and return an affidavit of eligibility and release of liability within 30 days of notification. In the event of non-compliance within this time period, prize may be awarded to an alternate winner. Any prize or prize notification returned as undeliverable will result in the awarding of the prize to an alternate winner. By acceptance of their prize, winners consent to use of their names, photographs or other likenesses for purposes of advertising, trade and promotion on behalf of Torstar Corporation without further compensation, unless prohibited by law.

This Sweepstakes is presented by Torstar Corporation, its subsidiaries and affiliates in conjunction with book, merchandise and/or product offerings. Prizes are as follows: Grand Prize—$1,000,000 (payable at $33,333.33 a year for 30 years). First through Sixth Prizes may be presented in different creative executions, each with the following approximate values: First Prize—$35,000; Second Prize—$10,000; 2 Third Prizes—$5,000 each; 5 Fourth Prizes—$1,000 each; 10 Fifth Prizes—$250 each; 1,000 Sixth Prizes—$100 each. Prizewinners will have the opportunity of selecting any prize offered for that level. A travel-prize option if offered and selected by winner, must be completed within 12 months of selection and is subject to hotel and flight accommodations availability. Torstar Corporation may present this sweepstakes utilizing names other than Million Dollar Sweepstakes. For a current list of all prize options offered within prize levels and all names the Sweepstakes may utilize, send a self-addressed stamped envelope (WA residents need not affix return postage) to: Million Dollar Sweepstakes Prize Options/Names, P.O. Box 7410, Blair, NE 68009.

For a list of prizewinners (available after July 31, 1994) send a separate, stamped self-addressed envelope to: Million Dollar Sweepstakes Winners, P.O. Box 4728, Blair NE 68009.

SWPS693

Wedding bells ring in our celebration of love and marriage. And *You're Invited!* Be our guest as five special couples find the magic ingredients for happily-wed-ever-afters! Look for these wonderful stories by some of your favorite authors...

Something Old—Toni Collins #941
Adrian Lacross was handsome and so romantic. How could Gabriella Thorne resist? If only he wasn't...a vampire! Could Gabriella's love make Adrian a new man?

Something New—Carla Cassidy #942
Eve Winthrop was shocked when the new principal showed up on a motorcycle. But Brice Maxwell dared to shake up his new students—and to take Eve for a ride on the wild side.

Something Borrowed—Linda Varner #943
Brooke Brady was on the yellow brick road to a new life when a tornado blew her car onto Patrick Sawyer's property. Was Patrick a heartless Tin Man—or a misunderstood Wizard?

Something Blue—Jayne Addison #944
Newly divorced, Quinn Barnett and Tony Falco found they were going to share more than memories—parenthood. Their baby seemed a miracle—and a message to give love another chance.

Lucky Penny—Elizabeth August #945
Dr. Reid Prescott didn't want love, but he needed a wife. Celina Warley was single and longed for a child. They weren't looking for vows of love...but with luck, would love find them? WED-A

Silhouette

R O M A N C E ™